MW01181772

The Scar Dance

BY

WILLIAM MANSFIELD

ECKHARTZ
PRESS

Copyright © 2018 by William Mansfield

Published in the United States by
Eckhartz Press
Chicago, Illinois

All rights reserved.
No part of this book may be used or reproduced in any manner whatsoever without written permission except in the case of brief quotations embodied in critical articles and reviews.

ISBN: 978-1-7323490-7-0

This is a work of fiction. While the author has experienced events similar to those depicted, the characters, events and all incidents described in this work are the products of the author's imagination.

This book is dedicated to my wife Anne who survived a terrible traumatic near death experience with tremendous courage, grace, and even humor. Having watched her come so close to death, I am grateful every day that she is my partner in life.

PROLOGUE

The huge bull mastiff leapt up and lunged to his right, slamming his paws against our wood panel fence. The fence shook from the impact, rattling our metal front gate. This was a distinctive gesture of the dog, which he made regularly when he saw me. He was among three dogs our next-door neighbors owned, including another huge bull mastiff, with similar grey brown brindle coat and a white pattern on its muzzle, and a smaller yellow dog which looked like a Labrador. The bull mastiffs were very tall dogs, with the long legs of a mastiff and the square head and muzzle seen on a pit bull and were estimated at over 130 pounds each.

I had just arrived home from work after a stop at the grocery store. I parked my car on the street in front of our neighbor's house, and unloaded the groceries on the street side of my car rather than on the sidewalk in front of their house, placing the car between me and the dogs. I often did this when these dogs were out, because they were very intimidating. Passersby often crossed to the other side of the street to avoid them.

As I was putting the groceries away in our kitchen I asked my wife Anne, "Are you still going over to meet our neighbor tomorrow about watching her dogs? I'm worried about you going over there! I'm afraid those dogs might be dangerous!"

The dog owners were a married couple who lived next door to us in the house directly to the east. We lived in a Chicago neighborhood called Humboldt Park, and we were friendly with them and we did each other small favors when needed. The neighbor wife had asked Anne to feed her dogs and let them out while she was the hospitalized for a medical procedure.

"Yes, I'm meeting her tomorrow afternoon," Anne replied. "I understand what you're saying. That's why I'm going over with the dog owner present. It's a trial run to let the dogs get familiar with me, and to see how they react to me. If there are any problems and I don't feel comfortable, I won't go watch them by myself."

“Ok,” I said, with audible skepticism in my voice. “Just remember what those dogs did to Alice when she stuck her nose under the fence for five seconds. Just imagine what damage they could do when they are in full flight!”

Alice was one of our two dogs, a small Kerry blue terrier with thick curly black fur. In April, a couple of months earlier, there was an incident where Alice had stuck her nose under a gap in the fence to the neighbor’s yard. Ironically, Anne was working on repairing that very gap, and had removed a temporary board as she was preparing to screw in a permanent board to close it. This gave Alice just enough time to put her nose under the gap, and one of the pit bull/mastiffs slashed her nose with a nasty gash that required us to take her to the emergency vet. The red gash stood out in bright relief against her thick black fur. I was not home when this incident happened, and when I got home, Anne was very upset, and there were spatters of blood all over the back steps and kitchen. We had to take Alice to an emergency vet on a Sunday. Afterward, she had to wear a white plastic cone on her neck, which covered her face and prevented her from scratching her wound, which required several stitches.

The next morning, after I told Anne I was worried about her watching the neighbor’s dogs, she and I left for work at the same time. She planned to go over and visit the dogs and their owner after work later that afternoon. It was a sunny Thursday morning, and as I kissed her goodbye, I said, “I’m still anxious about you watching those dogs!”

THE OTHER SIDE OF THE DOOR

"The door's unlocked," the dog owner wife called from a back room of her house. "Come on in."

Anne had just texted her that she was coming over, on a warm, bright afternoon, standing in front of her front door shortly after 1pm. The sun glistened off her bright red hair and light white skin. Anne was in a good mood because it was the first day of her summer vacation from her art teaching job. She had worked a half day that morning, and came home from work around lunch time, ready to start her break. The school year had been very tough for her, for both personal and professional reasons, and she was really looking forward to her time off. She had been through a teachers' strike, and then lost her job in the spring, due to school closings. She had a line on a new job for the following fall which she was optimistic about. She also had been through five failed rounds of IVF in the previous couple of years, the end result of which was three miscarriages. The third and final miscarriage was earlier in the spring. Besides IVF, we had also done several preliminary interviews with adoption agencies, and we planned to make a final decision that summer about whether or not we wanted to adopt a child.

So Anne was long overdue for some time off to take care of herself. She had several summer projects she was excited about, including gardening, making jewelry, and working out to get back in shape after IVF. Borrowing a phrase from a Seinfeld episode, we both liked to say that the summer would be *"The Summer of Anne."* When the neighbor called for her to come inside, Anne turned the door knob and opened the door. Immediately, the three dogs charged out and attacked her.

When the dogs lunged out the door, Anne immediately spun to her right to where there was a waist-high brick balcony on the porch. For a split second, she thought about jumping over the balcony to escape from the dogs, but she realized she might break a leg or ankle and be in even more danger. This thought flashed through her mind with lightening speed and before she could react farther the largest dog bit Anne on her right hip and buttock, locked his jaws, and dragged her down the front steps into the front yard, where both dogs ripped into her. It was the largest and oldest dog that initiated the attack, and he inflicted the most damage with the bite wounds. He was the pack leader, and the other two dogs followed suit when he attacked.

The front steps were solid, rough concrete, and Anne's body and head banged against the steps as the dogs dragged her down. She landed in a seated position on the front patio, trying desperately to push herself back with her arms while the dogs mauled her legs and feet. The most aggressive dog was huge, with massive mouth and teeth, which were ravaging Anne's left thigh. Anne was somehow able to turn and roll, and when the dogs got her on the ground in the front yard she was laying on her stomach. Basically a dirt patch, the front yard was torn up from the large dogs leaping around in it, wiping out any grass or other plants. The dogs viciously mauled Anne in the front yard, inflicting terrible bite wounds on her back, shoulders, ear, and worst of all, on both thighs. Anne desperately clawed at the ground, trying to crawl away from the dogs, while screaming at the owner to get them off her. She experienced the most extreme feeling of primal terror, with large vicious animals attacking her. When Anne rolled over on her stomach the pack leader immediately lunged for her neck, instinctively going for her throat in an obvious attempt to kill her. He lifted her off the ground by her neck, and Anne screamed at the dog owner wife, "I'm going to die! Get your fucking dogs off me! I'm going to die!" The wife wrestled with the dogs to get them off of Anne and after a major struggle managed to get all three inside her house, but not before the dogs had severely injured Anne, inflicting major bite wounds.

The neighbors heard the screams and the dogs barking and growling, and they rushed out to see what was happening. Anne was able to stand up, and she was drenched in her own blood, her clothes hanging off her in ripped, tattered rags. Every neighbor who was home came out in the street, and frantically called 911. There were numerous 911 calls recorded, because the neighbors called multiple times to make sure the ambulance arrived as soon as possible. One man was so worried that paramedics would not arrive soon enough that he offered to drive Anne to the hospital. She declined his offer, because she did not want to soil his car with all the blood. "Maybe you could put plastic trash bags down on my car seat and drive my car," Anne suggested to him.

When Anne stood up, she saw another neighbor standing behind the fence next door holding her cell phone, a Puerto Rican woman who had been one of the many 911 callers.

"What should I do?!" Anne asked her. The woman gestured repeatedly pointing to the front gate, and she hissed in a low voice, "Just get out!" Anne staggered out beyond the dog owner's fence onto the front sidewalk.

When this all occurred, I was at work doing inventory in a storage vault. My cell phone rang and I saw that the call was from Anne. Incoherent screaming was the only thing I heard when I answered the call. The tone in Anne's voice really put me on edge, and I was trying to understand her, and through the screaming, I could make out the words "dog attack" and "dog bite."

"I can't understand you!" I shouted back into the phone. "Are you ok?!"

"NO I'M NOT OK!" Anne screamed back in a shrill, panicked tone of voice. When I received the frantic cell phone call from Anne I knew immediately where she was and what she had been doing and I had a terrible feeling in my gut that my worst fears had been realized. I feared that Anne was going to die! I immediately dropped everything at work and rushed home.

Driving home from work, I received a call on Anne's cell phone from our neighbor who owned the dogs. She was hysterical and upset, and was apologizing profusely.

"I knew your dogs were dangerous!" I yelled at her on the phone. "I told Anne not to go over there!" She promised that the dogs would be removed from their property as soon as possible. I drove as fast as I could to get home, racing up Grand Avenue in Chicago desperately worried about Anne and dreading what I would find when I arrived.

When I pulled onto our block, I saw many people out in the street, including police, fire, and ambulance personnel and a number of neighbors. The fire truck was parked diagonally blocking the end of the street, and the ambulance was in front of our house, both with their lights flashing. I slammed my car into a parking space at the far end of our block, leaping out and sprinting down the block toward the ambulance.

Our dog-owning neighbor screamed when she saw me, "I'm sorry Drummond! I'm sorry!" She was standing next to the ambulance, crying hysterically. Her shins scraped up and dirty, her long black hair disheveled, and her round face was contorted with tears. At that moment, I was only concerned with Anne's survival, so I ignored her, and ran around the opposite side of the ambulance to avoid her.

"I'm Anne's husband!" I yelled to the ambulance drivers. "Is she going to live!?" Anne had already been loaded into the ambulance, and I could vaguely see her through the open door, under a blanket and wrapped in gauze bandages. She appeared to be unconscious and she did not acknowledge me in any way.

"She's going to live," the ambulance drivers assured me. "The dog bites just missed major arteries in her thighs and neck. Otherwise, she would have been in serious danger of bleeding to death." They also told me that their preliminary assessment determined that there was no long-term damage to Anne's nerve system or muscle structure. Next to the ambulance was a wheelchair covered in blood, which they had apparently used to move Anne. An EMT was hosing it off, and into the storm drain went the water, stained pink from Anne's blood.

Besides the ambulance, the police and fire departments had also been called, and two police officers were talking to our neighbor outside her house. I approached the police officers and told them I was the husband of the victim, and asked them if I needed to make a statement. Both officers were women who said they were friends with our neighbor. They said they had previously been over to visit her and her dogs, and had no problems with them.

"Shit happens," one of the officers said.

"We've had some other problems with these dogs," I said, and started to tell them about the incident where they slashed Alice's nose. Before I could finish my story, the officers waved me off and walked away and they continued to talk to our neighbor out of my earshot.

"Do you need any sort of statement from me?" I asked the officers when the ambulance was ready to leave.

"No, just go!" the officers said, again waving me off and walking away from me to talk to our neighbor. I found their attitude toward me to be very disturbing, and I did not know what to make of it. I assumed that since I was the husband of the attack victim they would want a statement from me, but they seemed much more concerned with talking to our neighbor who owned the dogs than with talking to me. For the moment I shrugged off the feeling of unease because I had more immediate issues to deal with, namely rushing to the hospital to find out how Anne was doing.

Before I left for the hospital, I went into our house to make sure everything was shut off and locked. The door was open and I saw that both of our dogs, Pandora and Alice, were in their pens where we put them whenever we went anywhere. They were barking and yelping hysterically. I did not know if they had seen any of the attack, but they most certainly would have heard it, as well as the ensuing commotion with the ambulance and fire truck. Clearly, they were very upset and knew something was wrong, even if they did not know what it was.

The EMT's told me that they had decided to take Anne to a hospital on the southwest side of Chicago.

"I've never heard of this hospital." I questioned them. "Why don't you take her to Northwestern Memorial, which is closer and in our insurance network?"

"Because it is the best trauma the hospital in Chicago," the EMT's explained to me. "Because they are located southwest, they get many of the gunshot wounds in Chicago, so they know how to handle major trauma injuries." His explanation made sense, and I was too distraught to argue with him further, so I told him to go ahead. I was extremely worried that Anne was being taken to a strange place, unknown to me, and concerned with what would happen if I could not find her.

"Do you want me to come with you?!" The dog owner wife called out to me as I was getting in my car.

"No thank you," I replied curtly as I drove away, because I was too angry to be in the same car with her at that time. The EMT's gave me directions to the hospital, and I drove off with no idea where I was going, or how I would find Anne when I got there.

ANNE'S HOSPITAL STAY

"Don't run any red lights on the way there!" the EMT's told me as they gave me directions to the hospital, right before the ambulance drove away from our house. "She's in good hands."

Despite their advice, my drive to the hospital was extremely stressful, and I fought back feelings of panic. It was a struggle to think clearly about how to get there, because I was extremely worried about Anne and I had no idea where she was, and I was in shock about the attack. I felt overwhelmed because the city seemed so vast and Anne could be anywhere.

"Oh shit! The hospital's not anywhere near here!" I cursed to myself as I made a right turn onto Chicago's Ogden Avenue. The EMT's had told me that the hospital was on Ogden Avenue and I thought it would be easy to find because my employer owned a warehouse on Ogden. I had mistakenly driven toward my work warehouse assuming that the hospital would be close by, only to discover that it was miles farther south on the same street. Even when I finally found the hospital, it was confusing to navigate.

"Where should I park?!" I asked myself frantically. *"Where do I*

check in?! Which way is the emergency room?! WHERE IS ANNE?!"

When I finally found my way to the emergency room, it was chaotic, much like a scene from the TV show ER. There were stretchers with patients everywhere, with doctors, nurses, and technicians running around all over the place. I found a small window to an office to check in with an attendant, and was ushered into a small waiting area which was basically a hallway with a few plastic chairs, with crowds of people rushing past.

After a few minutes of waiting, a doctor came out to see me, a very tall thin young man with straight black hair and dark complexion.

"Are you Anne's husband?" He asked me and I replied yes.

"Anne is conscious and stable," He assured me, speaking in a heavy accent which sounded Indian to me. "You can come in for a brief visit with her. Soon we are going to put her under total anesthesia to clean and irrigate the wounds. The wounds are very dirty from the dog's mouths and saliva, and also have a lot of ground in dirt. This process will be far too painful if she is conscious."

The Doctor led me through a swinging metal door into the ER patient area. I saw Anne on a stretcher at the end of a long hallway, against the wall in a row of numerous other patients on stretchers. She was covered in a white blanket and wrapped in so much gauze she looked like a mummy. Only her face and hands were visible. She was conscious, but seemed extremely groggy, with her face very pale and her hair disheveled.

"I guess I should have listened to you," Anne said, weakly holding out her hand to me when I approached her.

"I'm just so thankful you are still alive," I replied softly as I squeezed her hand. After a few minutes, the doctor returned.

"We're about ready to get started on the wound irrigation," he told us and he escorted me into another waiting area while Anne was taken away to the anesthesia clinic.

After that, there was not much for me to do other than wait. I used the down time to return home and feed our own dogs and let them out. I realized that I would need to start notifying family and friends about what had happened to Anne. In particular, I needed to call Anne's mother Joanne and her sister Amy, and I was not sure who I should call first.

"I would call Joanne but she has bad hearing and has trouble understanding me," I thought to myself. *"I don't want anything to get lost in translation with a call this crucial!"*

For that reason, I decided to call my sister-in-law Amy first.

"Did you call my Mom yet?" Amy asked, and I told her I had not because of my concern about Joanne's hearing.

"Do you want me to call your mom or would you rather do it?" I asked Amy. She hesitated for a moment thinking it over and then replied, "I'll call her."

Later in the evening, I went back to the hospital and I talked to both Amy and Joanne again. Cell phone reception was weak inside the hospital, so I had to leave Anne's room and go outside in the hospital parking lot, which was dimly lit. The June evening was warm, humid, and dark, and I made the calls standing in the parking lot shrouded in deep shadows.

"Did the dogs injure Anne's face?" Amy asked me.

"No," I replied. "Somehow she was able to roll over on her stomach and protect her face, so there are no wounds on her face."

"This is Horrible! Horrible!" Amy kept saying repeatedly. She had no argument from me.

Later in the evening, the dog owner wife arrived at the hospital. I did not really want to see her because I was shocked and angry about the attack. We sat alone together in the ER waiting room and I felt tense and awkward but still attempted to be cordial to her. She was distraught, crying and apologizing, and her shins were scraped up and dirty from the wrestling match she had with the dogs trying to get them off Anne.

"My husband is blaming me for the attack!" she told me tearfully. "He's threatening to kick me out of the house!"

"Why is he blaming you?" I asked, although I did not really care. "You both own the dogs." After that we fell silent and the wife sat huddled in a waiting room chair quietly weeping.

A short while later, a hospital chaplain came in to talk to both of us.

She was a large African-American woman in a white nurse's uniform with a cross on the shirt.

"We should all pray together," the Chaplain said. She led us in a prayer where she, the dog owner wife, and I all held hands in a circle.

"Bless us, please, oh Lord, to find strength and forgiveness in our darkest hours," the Chaplain prayed. "Bless this woman to heal from her wounds."

Shortly afterward a nurse came in and told me the wound irrigation had been successful, but that I would not be able to see Anne until the next day, and she urged me to go home for the night.

The next morning, I let our own dogs out in our yard, prior to driving down to the hospital to visit Anne. As soon as I opened the door, I saw the dog owner wife out in her yard with the attack dogs. I was standing at the top of our back steps, and over our wood stockade fence, I could see their broad, muscular backs with brindle coats moving around the yard. A lightning bolt of anger shot through me. I had assumed that after a near fatal attack, the dogs would be removed from the property and impounded immediately, as standard procedure, pending investigation. I was beginning to learn that this was not the case. There they were!

"When are you going to remove those dogs!?" I shouted out to the wife.

"As soon as possible," she replied, "I'm looking into dog shelter options in Wisconsin which specialize in rehabilitating dog fighting dogs and others with major behavior problems."

I also confronted her about the two cops who said they were her friends.

"I didn't like the attitude of those two cops," I said. "They seemed more interested in talking to you than to me. It's not their job to be your friend. It's their job to protect citizens like Anne and me!"

After I said that my anger softened, and I said, "Look, we like you both. We're good neighbors we don't want to just stick it to you. But this attack is too serious to just let it go."

"I understand, I'll take the dogs in," the wife replied. She went inside with the dogs, and I locked up our house and drove down to the hospital.

While I was visiting Anne the doctors came in to change her bandages and inspect her wounds. Since I was not present for the attack, and had only seen Anne wrapped in bandages in the ER, I had no idea what the bite wounds looked like.

I was absolutely unprepared for what I saw when the doctors unwrapped the bandages to inspect the bite wounds. Both of Anne's thighs were covered with a ring of wounds, which were terrible deep red gashes that encircled both thighs. There were also serious gashes on her shoulders and arms, her calf, and one on her ear. Anne had a very fair complexion and red hair, and the lurid red gashes stood out in stark contrast to her ivory white skin. During the attack she had been able to roll over on her stomach to protect her face, so there were no puncture bite wounds on her face or front torso. However her entire body was also covered with bruises. Her left breast was completely black with a huge bruise, and there were many other bruises on the rest of her front torso and legs as well. The horrifying gashes and bruises told the story of the terrible violence the vicious dogs had inflicted upon her body.

I was shocked and appalled when the doctors removed the bandages and I saw the wounds on Anne's body for the first time. Besides the horror of the wounds themselves, the doctors had installed what they called pinwheel drains into the wounds. These were loops of dull yellow rubber tubing, the purpose of which was to keep the wounds open.

"Many of the dog bites pierced completely through Anne's flesh," the doctors explained to us. "The dog's teeth met in the middle. These rubber pinwheel drains are looped completely through the wounds to keep them from closing in on themselves as they heal. If the wounds close prematurely there is a major risk of infection and abscess, so the purpose of the pinwheel drains is to keep the wounds open and prevent that risk."

The pinwheel drains were gruesome being looped completely through the terrible wounds, and they sent chills up my spine every time I attempted to look at them. Some of them looped through the same wound holes, crossing over each other, weaving a dreadful tapestry across the skin of Anne's thighs.

The wounds themselves were a horrible sight, and the rubber pinwheel drains made them look even worse. I literally could not look at them! I looked down at my feet when the bandages were removed by the doctors. They were closely examining the wounds, with their eyes a few inches from Anne's legs, and I could not believe they could look at them so closely without blanching. I found it amazing that they looked at hideous injuries like this on a daily basis as part of their job while I was traumatized by it. Anne later told me that I repeatedly put my hand up to my mouth in a nervous gesture, and my eyes were wide with fear.

"I'm glad you are watching us do this," The doctors told me. "When Anne comes home you will need to change her bandages and inspect her wounds."

That made me realize I would have to closely look at the wounds myself, and I did not know how I was going to handle that. I developed a ritual at the hospital where I would force myself to look at the wounds, counting to five, in an attempt to get used to seeing them.

When the inspection was complete, the doctor re-bandaged the injuries, wrapping gauze around Anne's legs and holding them in place with medical tape. He was methodical about placing the bandages and tape, and it took him the better part of an hour to finish. I began to realize that taking care of Anne when she came home was going to be a huge job, and I became very worried about whether I could handle it.

When I went home for the night after first seeing Anne's wounds, I was traumatized, almost in shock. Prior to seeing her wounds I had understood that the dog attack was severe. But it was only after I had seen them that I fully understood the true magnitude of the attack and how horrible it had been. I had planned to do a lot of work around the house when I got home, in preparation for Anne's homecoming, but I was unable to function. I sat on the couch for hours, not moving or even turning on the television. I literally could not do anything other than sit and stare at the walls in a vacant stupor, because I was so traumatized by having seen Anne's wounds. I had never observed such a terrible sight in all my life. It was like a horror film made real. That these injuries were inflicted on the body of the woman I love made it that much worse, and I was incapable of processing it emotionally.

A couple of days later the doctors handed me a plastic bag which contained the clothes Anne had been wearing during the attack. They were blood-soaked rags which had been ripped to shreds in the violence of the dog attack. She had been dressed casually on that day, shorts, t-shirt and sandals. I would have to go through the clothes to make sure there were no keys or anything else valuable in the pockets.

I took the bag of clothes home and had to wait a couple of days before I could bring myself to look at them. When I was ready, I braced myself emotionally and looked through the bag. The blood had dried to a dark black color and the cloth was stiff to the touch. The clothes were stuck together in a black ball, and I carefully peeled them apart, looking for any items of value. I did not find any valuables, and the only thing remotely salvageable was a pair of sandals, which were spattered with blood but not chewed up. I decided not to clean and try and save the sandals, and threw the whole bag of blood soaked clothes in the trash.

I spent the next few days shuttling back and forth between home and the hospital. I would usually drive down to the hospital in the morning, stay to visit Anne for most of the day, and head home in the evening to take care of our dogs and other tasks with our house. I always felt bad leaving Anne at the end of the day, and I could tell that she did not want me to go, but I had to go home to take care of things. The doctors had strongly emphasized to me that their major concern was risk of infection, and I realized that I had a lot of work to do preparing out house for Anne's return.

During my drives back and forth I started listening to a song by country music star Emmylou Harris called *"Beyond the Great Divide."* I found it comforting because it began with the lyrics *"There'll be greener pastures, 'cross that borderline, there'll be new horizons, my darlin', far beyond the great divide."*

The song continued with the general theme of finding a brighter future on the other side. I had long thought that Emmylou Harris had the most beautiful voice of any singer in any genre. Her voice had a haunting quality that could bring a tear to your eye under normal circumstances but especially so under the terrible circumstances Anne and I now faced. This song seemed to give me hope that we would somehow survive this nightmare, and I played it on a continuous loop during my drives to and from the hospital. It was the only thing I listened to.

The next day, the doctors and nurses started insisting that Anne take a shower, because they were worried about the risk of infection. We worried a shower would be painful for Anne.

I made sure to get to the hospital early in the morning to get ready for Anne's shower. The bathroom was shared by Anne and her hospital roommate, and we got Anne up out of bed and slowly walked down the hall to the shower. Anne was a healthy woman in her mid-40s but she hobbled slowly and gingerly, like an elderly woman. She had an IV drip with a stand attached to her arm which needed to be wheeled down the hall with her, with a walker to help support her, and she was wearing the typical the hospital gown that tied and opened in the back.

We made it to the shower and turned it on to a very low, lukewarm setting to make it easy on Anne's wounds, and then I carefully helped her in. Luckily, it was not too painful for her, and she was able to do most of her normal washing without a problem, with a special cleanser provided by the hospital. Anne did need some assistance from me to aid with her balancing and to prevent falling, and a lot of water was splashing on me from the shower. I undressed down to my underwear so I could assist Anne without getting all my clothes wet.

One of the nurses had seen us going into the shower and scolded us, saying, "Nobody who is not a the hospital patient should be in the shower with a patient!"

This made me angry because I was just trying to help Anne, and I snapped back at the nurse saying, "Look, I'm trying to help my wife take a shower and I'm getting wet! She needs my assistance!"

Anne said that she saw a number of different hospital staff coming in and out of her room during her stay at the hospital, including doctors, nurses, interns and staff. This was disorienting to her, because she was so groggy on painkillers that she was easily confused. She began to think that the hospital staff had a particular interest in her case, and this seemed to be confirmed by a statement one of the doctors made.

The senior doctor was a white woman, thin and angular, who appeared to be in her 50's. She was supportive, and also a straight talker.

"Have you ever seen anything like these injuries?" Anne asked her.

"No!" The doctor replied. "In most cases someone with your injuries would be dead!"

This really hit home to us how severe the dog attack really was, because the hospital staff were no strangers to major trauma injuries, given the number of gunshot wounds they dealt with.

"I would be more than willing to testify in court about the severity of Anne's injuries," the senior doctor told us, if we needed her to do so. We were grateful to her for making the offer, because Anne had come within an inch or two of losing her life, and we needed someone with authority to testify to that fact.

THE ROAD TO HELL IS PAVED WITH GOOD INTENTIONS

“Happy anniversary!” I said to Anne as I handed her a dozen roses. I had just arrived home from work, and Anne was standing in front of the dog owner’s gate, chatting with them through the iron bars of their fence. Their dogs were milling around in their front yard, and the largest bull mastiff sniffed me through the fence as I approached.

“It’s our 15th wedding anniversary today!” I explained to the dog owners as I handed Anne the roses.

“Congratulations! That’s great!” they replied warmly, and we went on to have a good conversation about what it takes to keep a marriage together in the long term. Our anniversary was Thursday, exactly one week before the dog attack.

The dog owner couple was sitting in the sun on their front steps, a large woman with a round face and long straight black hair, and an average sized wiry and muscular man, with medium length sandy blonde hair and a close-cropped beard and mustache, and always had a cigarette in hand. In the background we could hear live Mexican mariachi music being played in the yard of the Ramirez family, our neighbors on the west side of us. Every summer they hosted large family barbeques where they played live music with their family band. Puerto Rican children played in a plastic kiddie pool at the other end of the block, splashing, laughing and squealing with delight in Spanish. The sound of fireworks and honking cars floated over from a few blocks away.

"Is Puerto Rican Fest this weekend?" The dog owners asked.

"Yeah, I think so," I replied. "I've seen the booths set up in Humboldt Park."

The Humboldt Park neighborhood was the heart of the Puerto Rican community in Chicago. Each year in June there were booths set up prior to the annual Puerto Rican Festival, selling towels and t-shirts displaying Puerto Rican flags. The Festival was a raucous party that took over the entire neighborhood. Fireworks would blast throughout the neighborhood from the Puerto Rican Festival in mid-June through the 4th of July, leaving a pall of grey smoke hanging over the houses. This was always a rough time of year for our poor dog Alice, who was terrified of fireworks and thunder, although interestingly our other dog Pandora was completely un-phased by them. Often, we went out of town at this time of year to ease Alice's misery. All these noises were the traditional soundtrack of a Humboldt Park summer.

Besides the large Puerto Rican community, the Humboldt Park neighborhood also had a significant population of Mexican and African American people. It was generally a blue collar neighborhood, which had started to gentrify in the mid 2000's when real estate values were rising. But gentrification had ground to a halt around 2007-2008 when the real estate market crashed, and so the neighborhood remained very blue collar.

I had always considered our block a microcosm of the classic American melting pot, with four distinct ethnic groups represented, living next door to each other and for the most part getting along well. Going down the row of houses on our block there was an African-American family, a Mexican family, a white couple (us), and then

Puerto Rican households down the rest of the block.

Humboldt Park had a tough reputation throughout the city, which was well deserved because the neighborhood had some rough areas of gang activity and gun violence. However, our block was generally a quiet oasis with only occasional trouble. This was largely because of an elementary school across the street from us at the other end of the block, which served to deter any gang activity and push that a few blocks away from us. Legal penalties increase when drug dealing, gun violence, and other gang activity take place near elementary schools. The worst thing that ever happened to us was that we had a couple car windows bashed in, but otherwise, our 14 years in the neighborhood had been mostly peaceful.

Besides us, the dog owners were the only white people to live on our block in years. They had moved into our neighborhood approximately one year before the dog attack. We lived on a block with a row of brick, bungalow style houses and they bought the house next door to us, directly to the east. They were blue collar Chicago white people, roughly in their 40s, with no children.

Anne and I had lived in Humboldt Park for 14 years, having bought our house in August 1999. We were both artists, and we bought the house as a living/studio space which was a major fixer upper. Anne was an abstract, experimental artist who had worked in a wide variety of media including fiber arts, photography, and printmaking. She had done an installation of cast paper sculptures in which the paper was laid over old dresses bought from thrift stores.

My own artwork was much more traditional, pastel or watercolor images in a realistic style. I focused on gritty urban landscapes, and was in the process of completing a memorial series of drawings about my parents entitled *"A Eulogy in Pictures."*

Anne and I both worked in the fine art business, Anne as a kindergarten through eighth grade art teacher, and me for a moving and storage company which serviced art collectors, galleries, and museums in Chicago and the surrounding region. We were an artsy looking couple. Anne had bright red curly hair, fair skin, and wore horned rimmed glasses with red frames. I was a thin man of average height, with long black hair just beginning to get a few streaks of grey, which I normally pulled back in a ponytail.

Before the dog attack we had an amiable relationship with the dog owners. We were not close friends with them, but we were friendly. We made small talk over the fence and did small neighborly favors for each other when needed. Our property was separated from theirs by an 8 foot wood panel fence which we had installed a few years earlier.

They brought the dogs with them when they moved in, and we began to have concerns about them immediately. The dogs knocked our front gate out of alignment with the pounding they gave to our fence by constantly lunging against it. In wet weather, their front yard was a mud pit from the dogs leaping around, and our fence was spattered with mud. Despite our concern about the dogs, we continued to have a decent relationship with the dog owners prior to the attack. We talked to them about their dogs slamming against our fence, and they offered to install an interior panel on their side of the fence so the dogs would hit the panel rather than the fence itself.

Although we were upset about the incident when their dogs slashed Alice's nose, we recognized that we had to live next door to them, so we resolved the issue with them amicably. We split the vet bills with them 50/50, figuring that although their dogs had injured our dog, technically our dog was on their property having stuck her nose under their fence. In the spirit of getting along, we did not file a report with animal control or take any other action. Our veterinarian had strongly urged us to file a report with Chicago Animal Control, but in the interest of friendly neighbor relations, we chose not to.

The dog attack happened because Anne was trying to do a favor for a neighbor, with the best of intentions trying to help someone out, and it certainly spoke to the old saying *"no good deed goes unpunished."* The dog attack was a terrible, tragic mistake. It was a good deed gone horribly wrong. It spoke to another old saying, *"The road to Hell is paved with good intentions!"*

ANNE'S HOSPITAL STAY PART 2

"Another weekend of gun violence in Chicago!" a news anchor said on the television in Anne's the hospital room, as she looked out her window which had a view over the emergency room lane. It was late on a Friday night, and all night long she watched a steady parade of ambulances streaming in to the ER, their flashing lights slicing through the dense, heavy night air. The hospital never slept!

Anne wondered if the ambulances were transporting any of the gunshot victims she was hearing about on TV and she shifted her attention between the TV news and the window outside. She was half awake throughout most of her long dark night, groggy and disoriented from the pain killers which put her emotionally on edge. She was afraid, alone in a strange, forbidding place, helpless with serious injuries, and she really wanted me there.

At the same time, I was home frantically cleaning and organizing our bedroom. The doctors had told me their major concern was risk of infection and they emphasized to me that Anne's environment would need to be very clean and sterile. This was a problem because Anne and I were naturally messy people under the best of circumstances, so the idea of bringing her home as a hospital patient with severe injuries was extremely worrisome to me. We were two messy humans with three dirty animals, two dogs and a cat living in the house, plus we had ongoing remodeling projects that were unfinished at the time. So our house was anything but sterile at the time Anne was scheduled to come home.

The timing of the attack could not have been worse in terms of our home living situation. We were in the middle of remodeling our main floor bathroom and were using our 2nd floor bathroom to shower. This was a relatively minor inconvenience when we were both healthy, but when Anne came home from the hospital, it became a major one.

A few weeks before the attack, we had discovered some mold damage to drywall next to our upstairs bathroom. We had ripped out the moldy drywall but had not yet replaced it. For Anne to shower we would have to maneuver her upstairs past the mold damaged wall and into the shower without exposing her to any contamination that would cause infection. I did a thorough cleaning of the upstairs bathroom, and the stairs and hallway leading to that bathroom. I focused on cleansing the pathway from our downstairs bedroom to the upstairs bathroom, and I worried that my efforts would not be enough to prevent infection.

Because of this, Anne never told me how frightened she was during her nights at the hospital, or how much she wanted me there with her. She knew that I had a lot of work to do preparing our house for her return, and she did not want me to feel guilty for leaving her, so she hid her fear from me. She hid it well because I never knew about it until she told me months later. In retrospect, it should have been obvious to me that Anne would be afraid in such a foreboding place, but I was so overwhelmed that I did not detect it.

Although the hospital was a foreboding environment, the staff was helpful and considerate to Anne. Because the rooms were so stuffy, one nurse would bring Anne fresh ice water every morning, in a large plastic mug with a logo on the side. She also brought Anne a fan. Anne came to really look forward to her big mug of ice water, as she found it refreshing. Another nurse always brought me a meal if I was visiting at the time she brought Anne her meal, even though officially she was not supposed to because I was not a hospital patient.

The hospital counselor presented us with the option of moving Anne to a long-term recovery facility separate from the hospital, a type of hospice, as a transition prior to coming home. I seriously considered it because it could be a safer and healthier environment for Anne to heal, and would take a lot of pressure off of me. But the discussion about it upset Anne because she badly wanted to come home. She desperately needed to be in her own space.

"You sound like you don't even want me to come home!" Anne said to me angrily.

"Of course I want you home, Sweetie!" I replied, stroking her hand as I tried to reassure her. "I'm just really worried about how I can take care of you since our house is so torn up!"

Anne soon became restless lying in bed in the hospital, and began to take regular walks down the hallways. Several times a day she would ease herself out of bed, bracing herself on a walker. Then she would slowly and resolutely trundle down the halls doing laps around her hospital floor, IV tube attached, the hospital gown flapping.

"Am I going to go home today?" Anne asked the doctor on her second day in the hospital, after he had finished changing her bandages. The doctor had a surprised, incredulous look on his face in response to Anne's question, which he quickly tried to hide.

"No, I'm sorry but you won't be going home today," he replied. "It's going to be a while."

For the first few days after the attack, we maintained an amicable relationship with the dog owners. We understood that however horrible this attack was, we still needed to live beside these people, and we did not want things to get ugly. They were promising us that the dogs would be removed, and that they would provide us with their homeowners insurance information. They seemed to show genuine remorse, and they even came to visit Anne on her third day in the hospital.

The hospital visit with the dog owners was tense and awkward, but we attempted to be cordial. They walked into Anne's the hospital room bringing her a strange looking potted flower.

"Hey, you look great!" the wife exclaimed to Anne when she first entered the room.

"You haven't seen her legs!" I thought to myself, but I held my tongue. The wife's tone of voice sounded falsely positive, an octave too high, as though she wanted Anne to look great to alleviate her guilt. The husband said little, his face set in a hard look of anger. It seemed clear to me that he did not want to be there, and I suspected that the wife had talked him in to coming.

"We like you guys, we like you as neighbors," I said to them. "We don't want to stick it to you, but this situation is far too serious to just let it go. I have to file a report with Animal Control."

"I understand," the husband replied, grunting his reply in a low tone of voice.

After four days a nurse announced to us that Anne would be released from the hospital later that afternoon. The nurse made a funny comment, when she turned to me and said, "I guess this means you'll have to send all the girls away!"

Anne and I laughed with the nurse and I joked back, "Are you sure you can't keep Anne a few more days? I was just starting to have a good time!"

On the way home, we stopped and bought Anne a cane which was purple with butterfly patterns on the stem. When we arrived home, she leaned on this cane as she hobbled unsteadily up the front steps into our living room, with me walking close behind her to support her should she fall.

Anne burst into tears as she walked into our living room and shut the front door, her shoulders shaking as she put her face in her hands. I had never seen her appear so vulnerable and childlike.

"You made it home, Sweetie!" I said in a soft tone of voice, lightly rubbing her back. "You're in your safe place now."

I think Anne felt like she would never make it home alive, and when she did it, was very emotional for her. She had survived and returned to her sanctuary where she could feel safe, and she broke down in tears because she was overwhelmed by the emotion of her return.

Our two dogs Pandora and Alice were in the kitchen behind a baby gate leaping and yelping with excitement.

"Oh my God there's my babies!" Anne exclaimed when she saw them. Pandora and Alice were very high energy. Pandora was a wire-haired tan colored rat terrier and Alice a Kerry blue terrier with curly black fur. We realized we would have to keep them away from Anne because they might jump on her and accidentally re-injure her wounds.

It was a joyful reunion. Anne greeted Pandora and Alice over the baby gate, with the two dogs jumping up, happily licking her hands.

After Anne greeted the dogs, we slowly and carefully maneuvered her into the bedroom. We closed off our bedroom so she could sleep by herself. We normally slept with Pandora and Alice on the bed. I could not sleep in the bedroom with Anne because Alice and Pandora would be too upset being separated from us and would be whining at the door all night. So, for six weeks I slept on the living room couch with our dogs, so Anne could sleep in the bedroom alone with no risk of them re-injuring her wounds, and she could focus on her healing.

In the early days when Anne came home from the hospital, it was a major production getting her ready in the morning. We were instructed to change her bandages twice a day, once in the morning when she got up, and again in the evening before she went to bed. We had to remove her first bandage in the morning and then get her upstairs for a shower. Her balance was weak and unsteady, and I would ascend the stairs behind her to try to catch her if she fell. We repeated the process coming back down the stairs. I would assist Anne getting into the shower, then sit in the bathroom until she was done, in case she had any problems. She had a special anti-bacterial soap issued to her by the doctor, which she was told to use to prevent infection. The worst aspect was that she needed to move her rubber pinwheel drains daily per her doctor's instructions, and this was excruciating for her and impossible for me to watch.

Once we got Anne back downstairs into bed we would begin the process of changing her bandages. I had to inspect the wounds for signs of infection, especially those on the back of her legs which she could not see easily. This was a very difficult process for me, because I never became fully accustomed to viewing the wounds. I had to get close to them to look for signs of discoloration, redness around the edges, and any sort of odor, all of which could be a sign of infection. Although I had recovered from the initial horror of seeing Anne's wounds, I still found them very difficult to look at, and I never truly got used to it.

Once the wound inspection was finished, we would place surgical pads over them and wrap them in a roll of gauze. I would hold Anne's leg up while she wrapped the roll of gauze around her wounds. Finally we would tape the gauze in place, using as little medical tape as possible as it irritated Anne's skin. I continued to be amazed at the doctors and ER staff who could examine the wounds with no obvious sense of discomfort. At home I always dreaded the twice daily ritual of changing the bandages, because it was so hard for me to look at the wounds. I made several runs to a medical supply store to pick up bulk rolls of gauze, medical tape, and surgical pads. We filled several trash bags full of used gauze, tape and pads it was amazing how much we went through.

"This wound worries me," I thought as I inspected one of the largest gashes on Anne's thigh. *"It looks red around the edges and is starting to smell musty, which is what the doctors told me to watch for."*

I kept this thought to myself because I did not want to cause Anne additional stress, but I was worried about possible infection. Plus, there was a follow up appointment scheduled in a couple days so we would get a professional opinion soon enough.

Anne's teaching friend Christine agreed to take her to the follow up appointment, which was helpful because it allowed me to go into work and start to catch up there. I received a phone call from Christine about mid-day on June 28th.

"Anne has been re-admitted to the hospital," Christine informed me. "She is ok, you don't have to worry. The doctors are concerned that she has developed new signs of infection and they want to administer stronger antibiotics which they can't do at home."

I thanked her for taking her and letting me know and told her I'd visit Anne after work.

I slumped in my chair at my desk feeling defeated, like I had failed at home care. We both had tried hard to make it work at home. Besides the cleaning of the house I had done prior to Anne's homecoming, we had been diligent about changing the sheets, pillow cases, and other hygienic issues. She was re-admitted to the hospital for three days, so she spent a total of seven days in the hospital between the two visits.

Much of Anne's the hospital stay was very painful. In particular the doctors had to move all the horrible pinwheel drains as part of their effort to prevent abscess or infection. Anne had tears streaming down her cheeks during the procedure. After she was released the first time she had a follow up appointment scheduled a week later, and she had a tremendous amount of fear and anxiety about it because she was afraid it would be equally painful. All week long, I could detect fear in her eyes whenever this appointment was mentioned, so avoided talking about it. I talked to the tall, thin young doctor who I had first met in the emergency room.

"These follow up procedures are very painful for Anne," I told him. "Is there anything you can do about that?"

"Anne doesn't want to take her full dosage of pain killers," the doctor replied. "She's very resistant to it."

"Ok I'll try to talk to her," I replied.

This was certainly in character for Anne because she disliked medication of any kind and always tried to take as little as possible whatever the circumstances.

"You should take your full dose of pain medication," I told Anne after I talked to the doctor.

"I don't like it!" She replied vehemently. "It puts me on edge and makes me nauseated!"

"I know you don't like the side effects," I replied. "But I still think you should take it, it's better than the alternative."

Besides treating the wounds, Anne also had to have blood drawn regularly. This was painful because the doctors always had trouble finding her veins, and the more often they drew blood, the worse the problem became. They had to stick her on a regular basis, and at one point had to stick her almost 20 times to find a vein.

Anne was courageous throughout her stay in the hospital, and I admired her ability to withstand the pain. I was amazed that she wanted to reduce her pain medication, because I knew that if I had those wounds on my body, I would be taking the maximum allowable dosage and then some.

"Bring me a fucking horse tranquilizer!" I imagined myself screaming at the doctors if I had those wounds. *"Right now!"*

I could hardly stand to look at Anne's leg wounds with the rubber pinwheel drains, so I could not imagine the horror she must have felt actually having those wounds on her body. She showed tremendous bravery and strength in handling both the short and long term aspects of her recovery.

After Anne was released from her second the hospital stay, there were weekly follow up appointments, which I needed to attend with her because she was unable to drive or walk unassisted. The follow up appointments were long, drawn out affairs. They were usually scheduled mid-morning but there was almost always a long wait prior to the appointment. I missed a lot of work during this time, both full days when Anne was in the hospital and partial days for her follow up appointments. This was bad timing because my main responsibility was generating monthly storage billing, and in June, my company was raising the storage rates for the first time in years. I was directly responsible for implementing this rate change, and I was missing a lot of work at a time when I really needed to be there.

The Ramirez family who lived next door to us became very supportive during our home recovery phase. We had lived next door to them for years and had always had a cordial and friendly relationship with them, but were never truly friends with them until we bonded with them after the dog attack. They were a classic multi-generational immigrant family. They had three generations living in their house - two grandparents who spoke very little English, a mother who spoke proficient English but with a strong Mexican accent, and a teenage son who spoke English like any other kid born and raised in America.

As we arrived home from the hospital after the second stay, the grandmother Mrs. Ramirez approached Anne and requested to say a prayer for her. Mrs. Ramirez took both of Anne's hands in hers and gave her a blessing in Spanish, calling her teenage grandson over to translate it into English for us. It was a beautiful moment to hear Anne receive this prayer in Spanish. Mrs. Ramirez was reaching across the language barrier to offer Anne her support. She and Anne gave each other a big hug when it was finished. The family also put her on the prayer list at the Catholic Church they attended.

The Ramirez family had regular outdoor barbeques every summer, and they started offering me food from the parties.

"Come on over!" One of the Ramirez brothers called out to me, standing over a smoking grill and waving to me over the fence. "There's plenty of food, come on over!"

I walked to their yard, and he loaded me up with a heaping plate of grilled steak, corn tortillas yellow rice and refried beans.

"I'm sorry to just take your food and leave," I said. "But I have to get back to check on Anne."

"Of course, I understand," He replied. "You must be overwhelmed." He added a couple cans of beer to my care package and said that I was welcome to stop by any of their parties to pick up another plateful. This was helpful because the home care for Anne was absorbing my time and energy, and it was difficult for me to cook for Anne and me.

Anne had a decreased appetite after the attack. I did some online research to find out about foods that promoted healing, and I bought her Healthy Choice and Lean Cuisine frozen dinners that I could microwave. But Anne ate very little of what I served her, and I worried that she was not eating enough to aid her healing. She was a very particular eater under the best of circumstances, mostly vegetarian, although not terribly strict about it, and the dog attack seemed to exacerbate her food issues. I talked to the doctors about this, who said they were not concerned as long as Anne was eating when she was hungry and choosing healthy foods.

Anne's rubber pinwheel drains were removed a few at a time

by the doctors during these follow up appointments. We were both worried about the removal of the pinwheel drains because we thought it would be very painful. We were pleasantly surprised to find out that the removal was relatively easy, with only minor discomfort to Anne. Basically the doctors just cut the rubber loops with a pair of scissors and slipped the drains out of the wounds. They were removed a couple at a time when the doctors thought the wounds were ready. The last pinwheel drain was removed in mid-August, almost two months after the dog attack. We were both excited when the last one was removed, because it seemed to signify that we might survive.

Anne's second stay in the hospital lasted three days. On the day of her second release we got her dressed, packed up her belongings, and we were standing outside her room with the nurse when suddenly Anne disappeared.

"Did you see where Anne went?" I asked the nurse.

"No, I didn't see her," the nurse replied shrugging her shoulders.

I set off down the hallways to look for Anne, and I found her walking past a set of portable wooden steps which were practice steps for rehabilitation patients, leaning on her walker, doggedly trudging forward.

"Damn you're too fast!" I said to her when I found her. "I can't keep up with you!"

THE GLOVES COME OFF

On Thursday, six days after the attack, I arrived home from work at the usual time around 6pm, and as I got out of my car a woman approached me and introduced herself.

"Hi, I'm Camila," she said extending her hand. "I'm your neighbor I live at the other end of the block."

"Nice to meet you, I'm Drummond. I've seen you before," I replied as I shook her hand. "You're the lady who has the kiddie pool, you host the kids pool parties every summer, am I right?"

"Yep that's me," Camila said. Her demeanor suggested that she had been waiting for me and wanted to talk to me about something, and I wondered what was on her mind. She asked me how my wife was doing. Anne had just been home from the hospital for a couple of days, and was resting inside in our bedroom. I gave her a status report on Anne's recovery.

"The husband took their dogs for a walk this afternoon," Camila told me, nodding in the direction of the dog owner's house. "They got off leash and killed another small dog on the sidewalk in front of my house. Some lady I've never seen before was walking her small dog down our street and his dogs attacked and killed it. She wrapped her dead dog in a towel and went away and I haven't seen her since. I wasn't home but my 14-year-old niece witnessed the attack."

"Did this happen today?!" I asked Camila in consternation. I was confused about what she was talking about, because my understanding was that the dogs were under quarantine, meaning that the owners were not allowed to take them outside their fence. I could not wrap my head around the idea that there had been another attack by these dogs only 6 days after they had almost killed Anne. I was thinking that she must be talking about a prior incident.

"Yes, it happened earlier this afternoon," Camila confirmed. We walked down the block and she showed me the blood stains on the sidewalk in front of her house, salmon colored stains on the curb. We walked back near the dog owner's front fence, which was a high black metal fence with vertical bars a few inches apart, typical of fences in that part of Chicago.

"A child could put their arm through those bars and get bit," Camila said, gesturing toward the fence. "That's dangerous!"

"Yeah, we have an elementary school at the end of the street," I agreed. "Lots of kids walk by here every single day. You have kids, and there are other families with kids on the block."

Suddenly, the dog owner wife burst out of her front door, yelling at Camila, "What are you talking about?! What are you telling him?!" Clearly, she had been watching us through her front window, and it had made her nervous seeing me and Camila talking and gesturing in front of her house.

"Is this true?!" I yelled to the dog owner when she came out. "Did they really kill another dog today?!" She confirmed that it was true and began to get belligerent and defensive.

"You're a dick!" the dog owner wife yelled at me, standing at the top of her front steps. That set me off, because I was already angry that the attack had happened, and it was outrageous for her to get belligerent with me and call me names. I was outraged that their dogs had been involved another attack less than a week after they almost killed Anne, and that the owners had disregarded the quarantine order to keep the dogs within their property. I felt it was an egregious insult to Anne and me that they had walked their dogs down the block with no regard for the terrible damage their dogs had caused to her. They seemed to be acting as if nothing had ever happened.

"How dare you call me a dick!" I shouted at the dog owner wife over her front fence. "You almost killed my wife, you fucking bitch!"

"All our friends and family are telling us to sue you!" I yelled, having completely lost my temper. "I'll sue you and take your fucking house!"

"Do it you fucking asshole!" both dog owners yelled back. By that time the husband had joined the wife was on the front porch, clearly having heard the commotion from inside their house. He descended down his front steps, out his front gate, and onto the sidewalk, coming toward me.

Uh Oh! I thought as he approached. He had a taught, tense, predatory energy as he came down his front steps, and I feared the argument was about to get a lot worse.

The dog owner husband was not a big man, but he seemed manic, wiry and tough, although not much taller or heavier than me. He had told us that he played hockey in high school, and used to do motocross and dirt bike racing. He seemed like a man who had regularly engaged in barroom fisticuffs. So, although he was not much bigger than me, I had no desire to tangle with him in a physical confrontation. On a visceral level, I was angry enough that I would have loved to beat the shit out of both the dog owner husband and his foul-mouthed wife. But on a logical level, I am a peaceful person who had not thrown or taken a punch since a playground fight in 8th grade.

I do NOT want to mix it up with this guy! I thought as the husband approached. Despite the heated emotions of the moment, I made the logical calculation that if we got into a physical fight, I was probably not going to win. I also realized that even if I did win, his wife would certainly call the police, and the last thing we needed was for me to get arrested when I needed to be home to care for Anne. A physical fight would be a losing proposition no matter how it turned out. All these thoughts flashed through my brain within the seconds it took the husband to reach me.

The dog owner husband parked himself six inches from my face and began to yell at me about the dogs. I could smell a strong odor of cigarettes and beer on his breath. He kept turning his head from side to side the way a lizard cocks and turns its head as it surveys potential prey. I do not remember much of the content of what he yelled but I do remember that he was full of rationalizations about the dog's behavior, and their handling of the dogs.

"Nobody on the block had gotten robbed since we got these dogs!" he shouted at me. He seemed to have some twisted idea that he was actually providing a community service by having these dogs on the block.

"That's not true!" Camila contradicted him. "My garage got broken into just last month!"

"Dogs have instincts!" he yelled.

"Yeah they do!" I shouted back. "That's why humans who own them have to be responsible for controlling those instincts!"

"It's over!" was the last thing he yelled at me. "We're taking responsibility! We're removing the dogs!"

"You guys need to stop this!" Camila screamed frantically in a desperate attempt to talk us down. "We all live on the same block! We need to get along!" I was getting worried that our argument would explode into physical violence. I realized that I would need to talk the dog owner husband down, because I did not want a physically violent confrontation.

"I think if we get into it physically you would probably kick my ass!" I said to him. "But I think it's a really bad idea for us to get into a physical fight!"

"I know!" he said. "I'm not going to hit you." We walked away from each other and the fight finally began to calm down.

"I sincerely did not want things to get ugly between us," I said to both the husband and wife as I was walking back into our house. "I'm just really upset!"

"So are we!" they replied. But it was too late, the damage was done.

After the argument I went inside feeling extremely shaken, and I went into the bedroom to check on Anne. She was lying with a cream-colored blanket pulled up to her chin, propped up on a pile of several pillows. Her eyelids were heavy and her eyes were half closed, and she seemed to be drifting in and out of sleep. She was still physically incapacitated from her wounds, and on strong pain killers and antibiotics which dulled her awareness.

"You were outside for a long time," she said in a groggy tone of voice. "What have you been doing?"

Oh my God, Anne didn't hear the fight! I exclaimed to myself. *She has no idea what just happened! Should I tell her?!*

Anne had been sealed up in our bedroom and had heard nothing. I had an agonizing mental debate about whether I should tell Anne about the argument. I desperately wanted to not tell her, because it would ratchet up her stress level, when I wanted her to peacefully lie in bed and focus her energies on trying to heal. But I also understood that the fight with the dog owners was a huge new development which had completely changed our relationship with them.

You have to tell her about it! I told myself. *This is too big a development for you not to tell her!* There was no way I could not tell Anne about it no matter how much I wanted to protect her from it.

"I have something to tell you, but I don't want to," I said to Anne as I sat down on the edge of our bed, putting my hand on her foot. "I just got into a huge shouting match with the dog owners! It was bad! It got really ugly!"

I proceeded to tell Anne what had happened, with my hands trembling. Once I had finished telling her about the fight I was still extremely upset. To her credit, she handled it well, even in her condition, and she was calm and composed.

"You were right to tell me," Anne replied. "I really think you need to call someone for support! I can see you're still so upset!"

"I agree," I replied. "But who should I call?"

Given the craziness of the situation, we were not sure who I should call, or which of our friends could handle it and give us the best advice. We went through the list of our friends and family, deliberating who would be the right person to call.

"I think you should call Dylan," Anne finally decided. "He's a tough guy and he might be able to help you."

Dylan was an old college friend who I had known for 30 years, a writer, poet, and a fellow tennis enthusiast. But most importantly, Dylan was a tough guy who grew up in Chicago. He used to work in City Hall under the Mayor Daley administration, and he understood the gritty side of the city, both on the streets and in Chicago politics, so we decided he was the best person to call. I called and he was not home, so I left him a voicemail describing the fight.

"I'm sorry to get emotional on your voicemail!" I said, choking up on the verge of tears as I left him my message. "Just please call me, because I don't know what to do!" I sent him a follow up email saying the same thing. A short while later, Dylan called me back and he sounded furious.

"9-1-1!" he yelled into the phone shouting out the numbers slowly but forcefully, with a space between them for emphasis. "I want you to call 9-1-1! I want the police on your front porch in five minutes!"

"I can't believe those assholes got in your face after their dogs almost killed Anne!" Dylan continued with no abatement in his fury. "They're lucky you are who you are, because a lot of people would take out those dogs with a shotgun!"

I found my friend's anger to be comforting, although we did not take his advice to call 911. The fight was over, and it would be our word against the dog owners, so we figured there would nothing the police could really do. However, I found it reassuring that someone was outraged on our behalf and wanted to protect us. I put Dylan on speaker phone because I wanted Anne to hear him, and she found his anger comforting as well.

"Thank you so much!" I said to Dylan at the end of our conversation. "I could have called a lot of people tonight, but I called you. I'm glad I did."

MAN ON A MISSION

Anne and I renamed the dog owners Lizzie and Wade. When I first began writing this, I did not know what to call them. I considered keeping them completely nameless because they were dead to me, and being nameless seemed to symbolize that. I referred to them as dog owner wife and husband in the early drafts, but I realized that seemed awkward and cumbersome and I would have to find them names somehow.

Anne and I attended a performance of John Steinbeck's *"East of Eden"* at Steppenwolf Theatre in Chicago, which features a ruthless female villain name Cathy. This gave us the idea that we could name the dog owners after villains, fictional or real life. Anne did some on-line research of female villains and discovered Lizzie Borden who committed the ax murder of her father and stepmother in 1892. She was acquitted after a highly controversial trial which was a media sensation at the time. We decided Lizzie would be a good name for the wife.

I decided to name the husband Wade after a character in the movie *"A River Wild."* Wade was a criminal thug who terrorized a family during a white water rafting trip.

Two memoir writers gave me the idea of introducing the dog owner villain names immediately after my fight with the dog owners, where the relationship turns ugly and their true character is revealed. So, I kept them nameless until after the fight because until that point, we considered them to be friendly neighbors and this symbolized how we were unaware of their true character. The villain names Lizzie and Wade are revealed after the fight, and the dog owners will be heretofore Lizzie and Wade.

The night I had the fight with Lizzie and Wade had been a terrible one, and I was distraught, but over time I came to view it as a blessing in disguise. The second dog attack and ensuing argument provided a terrible clarity to the situation which I did not have before. Prior to the argument, we had maintained an amicable relationship with them, although it was tense, strained and awkward. After the argument, I was free to dispense with any of these pretenses. The fight had ripped the lid off a can of worms and their true character was revealed in stark relief.

I have always preferred my relationships to be well defined, and I abhor relationships which are fuzzy or ambiguous in the definition of roles. So, I felt better that the fight had given a new definition to our relationship with Lizzie and Wade. I had been uncomfortable with our awkward attempt to get along after the attack. I had been angry yet attempting to be cordial, and that made me feel conflicted. Now our relationship had a clear focus. Lizzie and Wade had become our worst enemies, and I could cut my anger loose with no inhibitions. I was furious about the attack and the subsequent irresponsibility from Lizzie and Wade, and I thought of a great quote from author James Baldwin. *"Hold onto your anger but use it. Don't let it use you."*

I understood that this was what I needed to do with my anger. I needed to use it as a motivational force, to give me energy, focus and determination during the upcoming battle.

The argument with Lizzie and Wade galvanized me and gave me a new sense of energy and purpose. I realized that we would need to take legal action, and I waded into the legal battle with tremendous energy and determination. It became my mission to achieve justice for the suffering they had inflicted on my family, and I threw myself into this mission with every fiber of my being. Prior to the fight, I had been in shock, overwhelmed and confused, struggling to handle the situation and take care of Anne. After the fight, I found a new strength and focus I had never experienced before. A work friend named Jeanine noticed a transformation in me and remarked months later, "You were unstoppable!"

This was a role reversal in my relationship with Anne, because in our day to day conflicts, she was normally the fighter. If we got bad customer service from a business, it was usually Anne who got on the phone to make a complaint, with me urging her, "just let it go; it's not worth the energy." I felt sorry for the hapless customer service representative on the other end of the line.

Anne was also a more aggressive driver than I am, and more inclined to honk the horn at other drivers. If I was driving and she felt I was being too passive she would sometimes reach over and honk the horn. I found this to be the most annoying habit on the planet.

Although Anne could be feisty, she also had an extremely big heart and a generous spirit. She displayed her emotions openly and honestly, a quality which made her family and friends love her so much, but also left her vulnerable to the evil and manipulative side of the world. Anne was not at all good at saying no to people, a character trait which had almost gotten her killed.

Anne and I had strong protective feelings for each other. If someone mistreated me Anne would often be angrier about it than I was and vice versa. I had never really felt that I needed to fight for Anne, because she was more than capable of advocating for herself. She had taught in the toughest schools in Chicago for 15 years, so she hardly needed me to protect her. But after the attack, she was weakened, physically, mentally and emotionally. She possessed a new vulnerability, so I began to feel that it was my job to protect her and fight for her.

It was out of character for me to charge into a fight like this. I am, by nature, a laid back guy who hates conflict. Standing up for myself does not come naturally to me, and many times I have let people mistreat me or take advantage of me without confronting them as I should have. As a teenage boy, I was the victim of severe bullying, which I never reported to my parents or teachers. Prior to meeting Anne, I had girlfriends who cheated and lied to me, but I never broke up with them like I should have. I had a history of staying too long at jobs where I was overworked and underpaid.

Over the years, as I matured, I gradually learned how to stand up for myself, but it was still in my nature to avoid conflict if possible. But with the severity of the attack and Anne's new vulnerability, this situation with the dangerous dogs and owners was obviously no ordinary disagreement. We were in the fight of our lives, and I was determined to do anything in my power to win that fight.

The morning after my fight with Lizzie and Wade, I awoke to the realization that I needed to take action. The first thing I did was to call Chicago Animal Control, and I spoke to a young woman who sounded like a receptionist or other relatively low level employee. I detailed the situation and emphasized how severe it was. I described both attacks to her with an impassioned plea that someone pay attention. I had previously assumed that the proper authorities had been notified about the dangerous dogs, since police, fire, and ambulance had been present the day of the attack, but I came to the terrible realization that this was not the case. Anne and I, along with all our family and friends, had assumed that the dogs would be removed and impounded immediately after such a near fatal attack. We were shocked to learn that this was not the case and that the dogs would remain on the property indefinitely at the discretion of the irresponsible dog owners.

Apparently, my description resonated with the young woman because within a half hour a more senior Animal Control officer called back. I relayed the same details to him about the attack on Anne and the subsequent attack on the small dog, and he seemed stunned.

"You don't have to take my word for this, but these are extremely dangerous dogs in the hands of extremely irresponsible dog owners!" I explained when he called me. "You don't have to believe me, but please send someone to investigate this situation! It's vitally important to the safety of our neighborhood!"

"Wow!" the Animal Control officer said repeatedly under his breath as I relayed the details of the story to him. He seemed confused and surprised that it had not been brought to his attention immediately saying, "This case should have landed on my desk as a red letter, high alert!"

Later that afternoon, an Animal Control officer came to interview us and to take photographs of Anne's bite wounds. She was a middle aged white woman who said she would be retiring soon. She parked her van labeled Chicago Animal Control in front of Lizzie and Wade's house, and I came outside to greet her. I had watched for her and made a point to go outside and shake hands with her, because I wanted Lizzie and Wade to see me and know it was me who called Animal Control. I wanted them to know that I was done playing games, and I was coming after them with any legal means at my disposal.

As I was doing so, a skinny African-American teenage boy in low slung athletic shorts was walking by on the other side of the street.

"Hey, are you going to get rid of those dogs?!" he shouted to the Animal Control officer. I loved hearing this because it showed me that other people in the neighborhood were concerned about the dogs. This kid did not even live on our block, but he still knew about the dogs and the danger they posed.

We gave the officer a series of photographs of Anne's bite wounds, which were gruesome, lurid images taken by both us and the ER staff. Anne downloaded and printed them herself even though it was difficult for her to move.

The next day, I arrived home from work to see our next door neighbor, Rosa Ramirez talking to a tall African-American man, looking around 40 with his hair just speckled with grey, wearing an Animal Control uniform with a tan shirt.

"I'm Officer Greg Johnson," he introduced himself to me as we shook hands. "I am going to be the lead investigator in this case."

Officer Johnson and I walked up and down the block with Rosa, and we both relayed to him the background of the situation.

"Those are the blood stains from the attack on the small dog," I told him, pointing to the faded but still visible salmon colored stains on the sidewalk in front of Camila's house. "Her niece witnessed the attack. She's 14 years old."

"Can I talk to her?" Officer Johnson asked.

"Let me call Camila. She's her aunt," I replied as I pulled my phone out of my pocket.

"I'm at a baseball game, I'm not home," Camila said when she answered. "But my niece is home. Go ahead and buzz my apartment if you want."

We pressed the buzzer on Camila's metal front fence three times, but her niece never answered. Officer Johnson also knocked on the gate of the Lizzie and Wade's home, but they did not answer.

"These are the gaps between the bars of their fence," Rosa told Officer Johnson, pointing to Lizzie and Wade's metal front fence, which had wire mesh on the inside blocking the gaps. The bars were a few inches apart, enough for an average person to put their hand and arm through the fence.

"They just installed that mesh after the attack," Rosa continued. "It was never there before. The dogs used to leap around in the front yard all the time. Little kids walking by from the elementary school would put their hands inside the fence. One of them definitely could have gotten bit!"

One of Anne's teaching friends named Christine had a great idea, which was to have a meeting with our neighborhood alderman to discuss all the problems we were having with Lizzie, Wade and their dogs. The alderman's office had an open meeting time from 3-6pm every Monday, so we arranged to meet with him on that day. I contacted our concerned neighbors and invited them to attend the meeting with us. It was Rosa, Camila, Christine and me. Christine did not live on our block, but she came to the meeting for moral support. Anne did not attend because she was incapacitated from her injuries, and had to stay home in bed.

We got to the alderman's office as early as possible, right at 3pm, and signed in on a sheet of paper where we put our names and provided a brief description of the issue we wanted to discuss. The office was crowded and chaotic, with a variety of people waiting to meet with the alderman for a variety of reasons.

After 30 minutes, we were told that the alderman was unavailable, but we could meet with his Chief of Staff. We were ushered to an inner conference room where we were introduced to the Chief of Staff named Maureen. She was a white woman who looked to be around 35-40 years old, with brown hair. She was cordial, and we proceeded to tell her the whole story of the dog attack and the background. Since I was the husband of the victim, everyone let me talk first out of respect, and after I finished, they weighed in with their details.

Rosa relayed some background information which I had previously been unaware of.

"I owned a small white dog named Lucky who was the pet of my teenage son," Rosa told Maureen. "When the dog owners first moved into the neighborhood, Lucky accidentally slipped through the fence into their yard, and was killed by their dogs. Since Lucky had gotten onto their property, and because I wanted to get along with our new neighbors, I didn't report the attack. We resolved the problem amicably."

"Wow, I never knew that!" I exclaimed. "That's very similar to our dog Alice getting her nose slashed by their dogs. We never reported that either because we were trying to get along with them, just like you."

"I guess Lucky wasn't so lucky!" Maureen joked. Then she immediately clapped her hand over her mouth and apologized, saying, "Oh my God! That was so rude! I'm so sorry!"

"It's ok!" The rest of us laughed and reassured her. "We get it we all thought it was funny too!"

Rosa told Maureen about witnessing my fight with Lizzie and Wade and how Wade's demeanor toward me was very aggressive. "I was watching from my front window with my phone in my hand ready to call 911 if it got any worse!" she added.

"Oh my God! I had no idea you saw the fight!" I exclaimed in surprise.

"It was really loud!" Rosa explained, "I could not have missed it!"

Camila described the second attack on the small dog walking

down the street, and explained how her niece had witnessed it. She also described Wade walking the dogs which he did regularly.

"He lets the neighborhood children pet those dogs all the time on his walks," Camila explained. "It's dangerous! I have kids two houses down from them and I'm worried!" She also emphasized the danger of the gaps between the bars of their front fence.

Camila described asking Lizzie how Anne was doing. "She shrugged her shoulders and scoffed *She'll live!*"

Christine spoke last at the meeting, and she got emotional in a good way.

"Anne is a really good woman who has fallen on hard times and she needs a break!" Christine said in an impassioned plea to close the meeting, with tears in her eyes. "She needs something to go her way! Please do anything you can to help her!"

"Thank you so much for coming out and supporting me!" I said to the three of them as we shook hands after the meeting, standing on the sidewalk in front of the alderman's office on Division street in Chicago. "Congratulations! You've done a good community service!" We all felt that we had done the right thing and had made a statement in confronting our terrible neighborhood situation.

At this point, we had been strongly advised by family and friends that we needed to find legal representation, and we set about seeking an attorney to represent us. We had never hired an attorney before, except for the real estate attorney when we bought our house, so we had no idea what to do. Fortunately I had two co-workers who knew attorneys through friends or family, sent me their contact information. I called both and made appointments for preliminary interviews.

I conducted phone interviews with both our attorney referrals, and arranged an interview with one attorney at our home. Both seemed very interested in our case, and I was hoping this indicated that we had a strong case. This attorney wanted to have an interview at their office, but I told them Anne was not up to it. We had to delay the introductory meeting for a week to give Anne enough recovery time to be ready for it. Since it was so difficult to get Anne to their office, they offered to come out to our home for a preliminary interview.

Our home interview was scheduled for 10am, and it was a struggle to get Anne ready on time. She was still incapacitated, needing assistance with almost everything, and it took a long time to get her showered and dressed each morning. Anne and I hurried to get her upstairs to shower, then change her bandages.

"They're going to be here any minute!" I said as I held Anne's leg up to dress new bandages, at 9:55am.

"I know, I'm taping these as fast as I can!" Anne said as she applied the medical tape to hold the bandages, while I held them in place. Just before the attorneys arrived we finally got her dressed and ready.

It was a hot, humid day when we scheduled the home interview. We had a high iron fence with a locking gate, which we left locked because of the security situation with Lizzie and Wade.

"Call me when you're out front," I told the attorneys. "I'll come out and let you in." They called me right at 10am, and when I came out to introduce myself they looked very hot, sweating in dark blue business clothes in front of our gate.

There were two attorneys who came to our home, a middle aged man who was one of the partners of the law firm, and a slim, young woman named Meredith with brown hair who looked thirty-something.

"Meredith is an expert on dog attack cases," the older man explained to us. "She volunteers for a dog rescue organization."

"That's how I know your co-worker," Meredith chimed in. "He volunteers there too."

The law firm specialized in personal injury cases, especially bike accidents. The older man did most of the talking, and was clearly the senior of the two.

"Most likely the case will settle out of court because most of them do," the senior attorney explained to us. "But there is a possibility that it will become a lawsuit and go to trial."

"Please give us the worst-case scenario," I urged. "If we do not settle out of court, and it becomes a lawsuit and goes to trial, how strong is our case?"

"Very strong!" the senior attorney assured us.

"I have an important question for you," I continued, and I explained to them about my fight with Lizzie and Wade. "I'm really worried about something I yelled at them during the fight. I threatened them, saying *All our friends and family are telling us to sue you! I'll sue you and take your fucking house!* Is that going to create a legal problem for us?"

"I guess I run with a rougher crowd that you do!" The senior attorney replied laughing. "I've heard a lot worse than that!"

I breathed a sigh of relief that nothing I said in the fight with Lizzie and Wade would cause any legal problems.

"Drummond's been so worried about this!" Anne told the attorneys. "I'm glad it's ok!"

The attorneys completed their presentation and Anne and I huddled together briefly in private to discuss whether or not to sign on with them.

"I like these people," Anne said. "In particular I have a good feeling about Meredith. I don't feel like we need to interview anybody else."

"Ok, I'm trusting your instincts," I replied. "Let's do it!"

The attorneys had us sign a form indicating that they would get 33% of any financial settlement awarded to us, and we were pleased to learn that it was done on a contingency; we did not have to pay them a dime unless we won a settlement. I liked them also and felt we had made a good decision regarding our legal representation.

The first step was for our new attorneys to contact Lizzie and Wade requesting their home owner's insurance information. We learned that the dog attack was treated legally as a type of property liability, and since it happened on the dog owner's property it was the responsibility of their homeowners' insurance company to provide compensation. We learned that the legal system viewed the dog attack as an accident, as if Anne had gone over to Lizzie's house and a tree branch had fallen on her, or she had fallen through a faulty stair railing. Anne had been the victim of a terrible violent crime, but the legal system did not treat it as a crime at all, merely as a liability accident.

THE SEARCH WARRANT

"How is Anne doing in the hospital?" my boss asked during my first day back at work, a large man with thinning red hair and a red beard sprinkled with grey. I had told him about the fight with Lizzie and Wade and my efforts with animal control to remove the dogs.

"Anne is being really brave." I replied, and I choked up on the word brave and burst into tears in the middle of an open office space with partitions, with several other people within earshot. I had not intended to be so emotional, especially in my workplace, but talking about Anne's experience in the hospital proved heartbreaking.

"I'm sorry, we don't have to talk about this," my boss said, kneeling and putting his hand on my shoulder as I was sitting in my chair at my desk.

"It's not your fault!" I blurted out through my tears. "I'm sorry to get so emotional! I want to tell you about it, but this whole situation has been a twisted, surrealistic nightmare! I wish I could just wake up from it!"

About a month later, another work colleague asked me, "Where are the dogs now?"

"They are still on the property," I replied. "They are still with the dog owners."

"What?!" She exclaimed incredulously, her eyes wide with disbelief. "You've got to be kidding me!"

"No, I'm afraid I'm not kidding!" I replied. The dogs remained on the property with the dog owners as if nothing had ever happened. These vicious dogs had almost killed my wife, and had killed or injured two other smaller dogs. There were three violent incidents involving these dogs, and yet over a month after the attack on Anne nothing had been done about either the dogs or their owners.

Our bedroom window faced directly toward Lizzie and Wade's house, and as Anne lay in bed trying to heal she could hear the dogs moving around in the yard next door.

A couple of weeks after we first met with Officer Greg Johnson, we received a letter from the City of Chicago Animal Control. It was actually addressed to Lizzie and Wade, but they had sent us a copy as well. The letter was a banishment order, saying that the dogs were banned from the city limits of Chicago, and that if they were found within the city limits they would be impounded immediately. Anne and I were thrilled to see this letter, and to know that the issue of the dangerous dogs had been resolved.

I also received a phone call from the alderman's chief of staff Maureen notifying me of the banishment order. I was elated when I got her phone call! It came while I was driving back to my office and when I arrived at work I did high fives with a friend Jeanine and my boss, celebrating our legal victory. Jeanine was my best friend at work, a slim woman in her thirties with straight, shoulder length blonde hair, highlighted with pink on the ends. I high-fived her so hard that I was afraid I hurt her hand. I was fired up because we had won the first round of our legal battle, and I was proud of myself for the role I had played in making that happen. I felt like I had just scored the first touchdown in the Super Bowl!

Unfortunately, this high was short lived, because Lizzie and Wade did not comply with the banishment order, and the dog issue remained far from resolved. They removed the dogs from the property for a couple of weeks, and we hoped that meant they were gone for good.

One Saturday afternoon in July, we looked out through our upstairs back window and saw Lizzie and Wade bringing the dogs back through their back gate. Anne's whole body was shaking when she saw the dogs, and I felt the urge to vomit. The largest bull mastiff, the pack leader of the attack, laid down in their yard, sunning itself with contentment, and the sight made us sick. We immediately called Animal Control and told the investigator that the dogs were back.

Finally, the dog case was turned over to an agency called the Police Animal Crime Team, who obtained a search warrant authorizing the seizure of the dogs. One morning in August we received an email during my work day from Maureen in the Alderman's Office, which said the following:

Drummond & Anne - I just spoke with Animal Control. Since Lizzie is not cooperating with their investigation they have turned this case over to the police. The Chicago Police Animal Crime Team will be at her house this morning by 10:30 a.m. to investigate whether or not she has returned the dogs to her home. If she does not cooperate, they can gain access to the house right there with a search warrant. If they determine the dogs are the same they will be seized. She can also be arrested if she does not cooperate. Animal Control will keep me updated and I'll share the info. with you.

My hands were shaking as I read her email, because I knew that this was ratcheting up the dog case to a whole new level. I was on a break from work at around 10am when I read the email. I realized that Lizzie would try to escape out the back with her dogs, because she had evaded Animal Control inspections previously with that maneuver. I knew this because Camila had twice seen Lizzie slipping the dogs out the back while Animal Control officers were in front of her house, and she had tipped me off about this. I rushed to call Maureen on her cell phone, and fortunately, she was available to answer.

"I'm so glad you're available to take my call!" I said to Maureen. "Lizzie is going to try to escape out her back door with her dogs! She's done it before with Animal Control inspectors! Please call your police contacts ASAP and tell them to cover the back alley!"

“Yes, I’ll call them right now!” Maureen replied, and we got off the phone quickly, so she could call the police. I also called Anne who was teaching at the time and left her a message about what was about to happen.

When I hung up with Maureen I walked into Jeanine’s office.

“Please keep your fingers crossed!” I asked Jeanine as I described the situation to her, with my fingers trembling. “Please keep your fingers crossed that the police will succeed!”

After that it all became a big waiting game. Throughout the rest of the day I obsessively checked my emails and cell phone call logs, but I found no new information. I was unproductive at work because all I could think about was whether or not the police action had succeeded. Toward the end of the day I called Maureen again, but she did not have any new information because her main contact at Animal Control was out sick for the day.

“I’m as anxious to know as you are,” She assured me. “I’ll let you know ASAP if I hear anything.”

Anne and I went home after work that evening not knowing what had happened, or if the dogs had been seized. We spent the evening on pins and needles with tremendous anxiety, wondering if the police seizure had been successful. When we got home we could sense that something was different next door, but we did not know what it was. We were on high alert, carefully watching the neighbor’s property for any clues. We did not see Lizzie nor the dogs. We were hoping against hope that this meant the police had succeeded, but we did not know.

We did see Wade out in their back yard, glaring at us as we went in and out of our house. He had his characteristic threatening look, where he would stand with legs apart, arms folded, glaring at us, and this evening he appeared especially menacing. He was standing in the shadow of their tall balcony, shrouded in the deep shadow, appearing ominous. His threatening attitude also made us think something had happened, but again what it was, we did not know.

Later in the evening, when we went inside we got a phone call from Animal Control.

"We have two dogs impounded," the Animal Control officer told us. "Would you be willing to come in and identify the dogs?"

It was a female officer from Animal Control, and her voice sounded like a young woman. She seemed tense and guarded, as though she was not authorized to give us additional information and had to be very careful about what she said. It seemed like she was holding something back. We agreed to come in to the Animal Control pound and identify the dogs.

We did not know what really happened with the seizure of the dogs until the next day, when I received a phone call from Maureen. I was shocked at what she told me about the events of the previous day.

"It happened exactly as you said it would!" she said to me. Apparently when the police had attempted entry into Lizzie's front gate with a search warrant, she had rushed the dogs out the back, into her car in her garage, and taken off down the alley. The police had stationed an officer covering the alley, and she had almost run him over as she fled down the alley. The officer had to dive out of the way to avoid being hit by her car. A police chase ensued down the alley, and the police eventually ran her down, seized the dogs, and arrested Lizzie. Both Maureen and I were stunned that Lizzie would take it that far.

"She is in a lot of trouble!" Maureen told me.

"Every time I think this situation can't get any crazier, it gets crazier!" I replied to her.

"Oh my God!" Anne exclaimed when I called her to relay the news. "I cannot believe this is happening!"

Lizzie spent a night in jail, and then was apparently bailed out because she returned home. Once she returned home, she was like a shrieking banshee, which was terrifying, because we had no idea what she was truly capable of. Two days after her dogs were seized by the police, we came home in the evening after work and as per our usual routine, let our own dogs, Pandora and Alice out in the back yard. Pandora barks a lot, and she started barking at something in the back yard.

"Shut your fucking dog up, you fucking assholes!" Lizzie screamed at us, rushing out on her tall balcony. Her voice had a bone chilling tone of pure hatred and fury, and it was clear that she blamed us for her dogs being seized and her being arrested. We took Pandora and Alice inside because we worried about what Lizzie might do to us. By this time, we were very concerned that they might possibly have guns or other weapons in their home. If so we were afraid she might come out on her balcony and start blasting away at us.

It was no accident that their dogs were dangerous. Lizzie and Wade wanted them to serve the purpose of being weapons. We believed that the dogs were dangerous because they were owned by dangerous people. There was no reason to believe that they did not own other weapons as well. Lizzie had almost run over a police officer, so it was obvious that there were no limits or filters on her behavior. We were extremely worried about what she would do next.

We took our dogs out in the front yard, hoping that Lizzie would leave us alone since the front yard was more in view of other people on the street, witnesses who might serve as a deterrent. This was of no use, because she opened her front window and started screaming at us again, with a crazed, maniacal tone of voice. We went back inside again to re-group and try to figure out what to do. We had to get Pandora and Alice outside somehow, because they had been inside all day while we were at work, and they needed to relieve themselves. Both dogs were frantically pacing around our house, clearly agitated because they were confused and could sense our fear. The house was silent except for the sound of their claws clicking rapidly against our hardwood floors.

"I'm scared shitless!" I snapped at Anne. "I don't know what the hell to do!" Anne and I had started to get into an argument with each other, because we were both frightened and on edge, with no idea what to do next. After much deliberation, we decided to call Maureen, who advised us to call 911 immediately, which we did.

The police showed up quickly and were very supportive. We were watching intently out our front window waiting for them, and at that moment there was no more beautiful sight on the planet then seeing that cop car roll up in front of our house. There were two officers, an older white man with military hair cut speckled with grey, and a younger Latino man with a round face and straight black hair. The older officer did most of the talking, and seemed supportive of our story when we gave him the background.

"This is strange!" The older officer exclaimed in surprise. "We never get calls on this block!" This was because our block had mostly been safe and peaceful for years, despite being in the middle of the rough Humboldt Park neighborhood. Before Lizzie and Wade moved onto our block, we had very few problems.

The patrol car was equipped with a computer on the dashboard, and we asked him to look up the record of Lizzie resisting arrest. Unfortunately, he was unable to find anything in the system about her. In retrospect we realized that we had given him the wrong last name for Lizzie, and that was why he could not find her in their system. The younger officer did not say much, and he quietly slipped out of the car and tested the front gate of Lizzie and Wade, asking us about the dogs as he did so. The gate was unlocked so he went inside.

"Where did he go?!" The older officer asked, urgently looking over his shoulder, because he had not seen his partner going in Lizzie and Wade's front gate. The younger officer knocked on their door and Wade came out to talk to him. We could not hear what they were saying but could see Wade gesturing as they talked. They were obscured by a brick wall on their front porch, but from behind the wall we could see Wade's arm gesticulating frantically, cigarette in hand.

"You're in big trouble!" the young officer said jokingly when he returned. Apparently and not surprisingly, Wade had lied and had said the bad blood between us was totally our fault. The older officer opened the trunk of the cop car, which contained some paperwork about how to file for an order of protection, a restraining order, and he gave us copies of this paperwork.

"Hang in there," the older officer told us kindly as they left.

Finally, after the police had left we were able to take our poor dogs out in the yard with no farther incident. Neither Alice nor Pandora barked, and they seemed to know that there was a problem because from that day forward they were always very quiet in the back yard. After this incident, we realized that we had every reason to fear for our safety from Lizzie and Wade, and we began to understand the gravity of our situation. We had made enemies with two people who were potentially extremely dangerous, and happened to live right next door to us.

THE LONG HOT SUMMER

"Who you gonna yell at now, you fucking asshole!?" Arturo Ramirez shouted at Wade. Several of the Ramirez family men had surrounded Wade, shouting at him on the sidewalk in front of their house. It was a Saturday night, and the Ramirez family was having one of their big barbeques they had every summer, with the family band playing live Mexican music. Each summer the Ramirez family had regular large outdoor parties with family and friends. They would always have live music, amateur musicians from the family who played traditional Mexican Mariachi music. Over the years the family band improved dramatically, and we came to really enjoy the music. It became a summer tradition for us to work in our garden on Saturday evenings, while listening to a free concert of Mexican music from the next door yard. We would clap and cheer over the fence when they finished a good number.

Apparently, Lizzie and Wade did not share our appreciation of the live Mexican music, because Wade had started a fight with the Ramirez family when he came out on his balcony and yelled, "Shut your fucking music off! We're trying to sleep!" One of the family musicians picked up the band's microphone and beckoned, "Why don't you come on out here like a man and say that!?" Foolishly Wade did just that, and several of the Ramirez men surrounded him, shouting at him, "Who you gonna yell at now!?" Lizzie called the police, who came out and talked to everyone involved, but there were no arrests, and lucky for Wade there was no physical violence. Anne and I almost wished that the Ramirez men would have kicked Wade's ass, but we also did not want any of them to get arrested or get in trouble, so it was for the best that they did not hurt him.

Anne and I were not home that Saturday night because we were house sitting for a friend in another neighborhood, so we missed all the fun. The story was later relayed to us by Arturo's sister Rosa, who also told us about another incident where Lizzie and Wade had yelled at her parents about where they parked their car. The older Ramirez grandparents did not speak English. Mr. Ramirez parked his car in front of Lizzie and Wade's house, which was perfectly legal since there was no reserved permit parking on our block. Lizzie and Wade came out and verbally abused him, shouting that he could not park his "fucking car" in front of their house. This was ridiculous for two reasons. Mr. Ramirez had every legal right to park there and he did not speak English so he had no idea what they were yelling. He had to go inside and ask the rest of his family what the problem was.

We appreciated that the Ramirez family openly supported us and that they would stand up to Lizzie and Wade, because their attempts at intimidation had been successful with other people on the block. Our attorneys had hired an investigator to interview people on our block about the attack, and he reported back that it was very difficult to find anyone willing to talk. So, we were grateful that the Ramirez family was not intimidated and were willing to stand up to Lizzie and Wade.

"Camila can't come to the phone," her brother told me when I called her one evening a few days after the alderman meeting. "She's busy cleaning nails out of her kid's pool."

"That's a weird answer!" I thought to myself as I put down my phone. A brief thought flashed through my mind that maybe Lizzie and Wade had done something to Camila and I had a creepy feeling in my

gut which made my skin crawl. I soon put it out of my mind because I was still overwhelmed with trying to take care of Anne, so I had plenty of other things to think about. A few days later, I ran into Camila who told me she had woken up one morning to find the bottom of her kid's swimming pool strewn with nails, drywall screws, box cutter blades and other sharp objects. Sometime during the night, someone had thrown these dangerous objects into her pool. She was convinced that Lizzie and Wade had done it to send a message of intimidation. I agreed with her. Unfortunately, there was no way to prove it because neither of us had seen them do it, but I had no doubt about the identity of the vandals. The incident made me think of the horse head scene from "The Godfather." If it was indeed Lizzie and Wade we all found it extremely disturbing that they would send such a cold, calculated message of intimidation, especially since it targeted Camila's minor children. Each new development opened our eyes wider about how dangerous Lizzie and Wade were. A cold knot of fear tightened in my gut realizing what ruthless enemies we had.

Camila also told me that Lizzie had come out on her tall balcony one afternoon screaming abuse at her, calling her a fucking bitch, cunt, and whore, all while Camila's young children were out in her yard to hear it. The balcony was becoming a dark opera stage for Lizzie's threats and verbal abuse. Anne and I had always thought their balcony was an eyesore, but after the attack, it also became a platform for their abuse. Lizzie also yelled at Camila, "You better not tell Drummond about this!" I found that last part interesting and it made me wonder why Lizzie would bring my name into it. I hoped that it meant that Lizzie was worried about me, that she knew I was taking legal action against her and Wade and it was causing her concern.

There was another Puerto Rican family who lived next door to Lizzie and Wade, on the other side from us directly to the east. During July, they quickly and quietly moved and were never seen again. Anne and I had never talked to them and knew nothing about them, but we could not help but wonder if it was more than a coincidence that they happened to mysteriously move at that time.

It was also disturbing that Lizzie and Wade not only hated us but also seemed to be targeting people they associated with us. It seemed clear that they viewed both the Ramirez family and Camila as our allies, and would target them as well as us with intimidation and harassment. After years of peaceful coexistence with our neighbors, Lizzie and Wade single- handedly turned our block into a war zone. This summer was turning out to be a long, hot summer.

The threat from Lizzie and Wade was exacerbated by the physical setup of our two residences, because the bungalow style houses in that area of Chicago were built close together. From the brick wall of our house it was only a few feet across a narrow gangway to our wood stockade fence which was the property line. From the fence it, was only a few feet across another gangway to their house. Overall, our two houses were separated by only approximately 10-15 feet. So, not only did we live next door to our enemies and their dangerous dogs, but our houses were close to one another.

When Anne was in the hospital for the second time, after my fight with Lizzie and Wade, I had to go home to the house alone after visiting her. I was terrified to go into the house by myself. I carried a short handled 3 prong garden tiller in and out of the house with me, in case either the dogs or their owners came after me. One of the first nights back from the hospital, I arrived home by myself after dark. I let our dogs out in the back yard and they disappeared, and I panicked, thinking something terrible had happened to them. I realized that an interior back gate had been left open, which separated the back yard from the front, where we usually kept our dogs in the back. Normally, we kept it shut and it was probably me who accidentally left it unlocked but I could not be sure at the time. I worried that Lizzie and Wade had broken into our yard and left the back gate open. I rushed around in a panic trying to find our dogs, and I finally found them huddled near the front door. I hustled them into the house, and then did a full check of every part of the house by flashlight. I did the same check every night when I came home from the hospital.

Not long after this incident, we found a note taped to our mailbox which was very disturbing. The note was typed, and was not named or signed. We did not know who wrote the note, and we did not see anyone taping it to our mailbox, but we strongly suspected that it was from Lizzie. We could not see how it could have been written by anyone else. Below is what the note said:

"So, in light of what I feel is becoming harassing behavior, I have taken a moment to research and print out the laws regarding trespass. Please read them carefully and note that I have up to five years to make a charge.

My friends that arrived at the scene of the accident, which is exactly what it was, an accident, asked me at the time, if I wanted to press charges and I declined in the spirit of being neighborly.

I have recently changed my mind regarding that topic as I am tired of being treated as a criminal, and as if I had done something wrong; I did nothing wrong.

Anne unlawfully trespassed into my home, and I will feel completely free to go ahead with charges if your harassment and your invasion of my privacy, continue. I seriously doubt she will find much work as a teacher with a criminal record.

I highly advise you to stand down and carry on with your lives and feel free to ignore us in the future, as we will feel free to ignore you."

Anne saw this note when Christine brought her home from one of her doctor's appointments, and she was shaking when she read it. Anne was furious that Lizzie would accuse her of trespassing, when Anne had gone over to her house to do her a favor and was almost killed in the process. The note showed us very clearly that Lizzie was a disgusting person who had no integrity, moral compass or conscience about her behavior. Luckily, we had anticipated the trespassing charge, and Anne had saved screen shots of her text message chain with Lizzie, where Lizzie clearly asked Anne to come over and watch the dogs. We had forwarded that text message sequence to our attorney, so we were well covered legally if Lizzie proceeded to file trespassing charges.

The one part of Lizzie's note we liked was about them and us ignoring each other. We were happy to comply with that, and we had already agreed on a strict policy that we would not respond to Lizzie and Wade, no matter what they did. We did not reply to her note, and we agreed that we would not respond in any way if they yelled threats or abuse at us. We would call the police if necessary but otherwise, completely ignore them.

This pattern of harassment and attempted intimidation continued for the next several months. One Saturday morning, not long after our big argument, I let our dogs out early, and one of them started barking at something. Wade came out on their balcony and yelled "Shut your fucking dog up!" I gave him no reply and took our dog back inside. Apparently, they viewed it as an equivalency that their huge dogs almost killed Anne, while our small dog did some annoying barking. I guess that evened it out in his mind.

In July, we were cited for overgrown weeds in our yard. We could not be sure who reported us, or if the City cited us independently, but we strongly suspected Lizzie and Wade. At the time, Anne was still incapacitated with her injuries, and I was overwhelmed with taking care of her and handling all the affairs of our house. So, yard work was our lowest priority, and we were reaching the height of summer growing season, and the weeds were growing tall. We awoke one morning to find a note from the City of Chicago posted on our fence, warning us that our weeds were overgrown and presented a safety hazard. We had 30 days to remove the weeds or incur a $500 fine. If it was indeed Lizzie and Wade who reported us it was pathetic that they would be petty and vindictive enough to report us for tall weeds, when they had been the ones to victimize us to begin with.

We were fortunate to have supportive friends, and two of Anne's teaching friends came over with trimmers, and we spent a weekend hacking down all the weeds. Anne felt bad because she was unable to help much, as she was still weak from the bite wounds. She had to just sit in a chair in our back yard and watch, trimming a few weeds as much as she could.

We lived with a siege mentality in July and August. Because of the threat from Lizzie and Wade, we were on high alert during every trip in and out of the house, and the stress level was excruciating. Even when there was no incident, we were hyper-vigilant that something might happen, and it was exhausting to constantly be on guard in our own home. Whenever I came home from work, I would call Anne as

I turned onto our block, and she would watch me from the front door as I walked in, with her cell phone in hand in case she needed to call 911. Anne did not go in and out of the house alone, period. We went to the alderman's office and obtained several signs that stated *"We Call Police"*, and I wallpapered our house with them. I taped three in our windows directly facing the dog owner's house, and four more facing either the street or back alley. It was a horrible way to live, in a constant state of fear and high tension in our own home and yard. Every day when I came home from work I could feel the muscles in my jaw and shoulders tighten with tension as I turned down our street.

Our block was always crowded with children and their parents when the elementary school let out in the afternoon. One day, Anne was trying to turn our car around, struggling to do so because the street was so crowded. She looked up and saw Lizzie standing in her front window, pointing at Anne and laughing maniacally. We could not even do the most ordinary tasks without Lizzie obsessively watching us.

Another day, I ran out to do some errands while Anne was cleaning upstairs in the house, and when I returned, she had locked the screen door and I could not get in. I tried calling her repeatedly but she did not answer. I started to panic at being stranded outside, fully aware that Lizzie was probably watching me. Finally, I gave up calling, grabbed a stick and punched a hole in the screen so I could reach through and unlock the door from the inside.

"Why didn't you answer your fucking phone?!" I angrily snapped at Anne when I finally got inside.

"I didn't hear it!" She replied. "I was upstairs cleaning the bathroom with the water running." It was amazing how a minor misunderstanding could escalate into a crisis because of the threat from Lizzie and Wade.

In retrospect I have no idea how we even survived this living situation. I credit the fact that you find strength when there is no alternative. Our backs were to the wall, and we had no choice other than to be strong and confront our terrible situation or have an emotional meltdown and completely fall apart. Certainly, these circumstances made it impossible for Anne to begin properly healing. Our bedroom faced in the direction of the dog owners house, and as she lay in bed trying to heal, Anne could hear the dogs that attacked her barking and moving around in their yard. We had a piece of plywood which we screwed in over the bedroom window to prevent burglaries whenever we went out of town. We would normally remove it when we were back in town. After things got ugly with Lizzie and Wade, we left the plywood in place permanently. We attached Anne's get-well cards to the plywood with thumbtacks.

In August, we installed security cameras on our house, to the tune of $1,500. We were struck by the fact that we had lived in the Humboldt Park neighborhood for 14 years with no need for security cameras, even though the neighborhood had gang activity and gun violence. But because of Lizzie and Wade, we installed security cameras. The installation itself was stressful because we thought the security cameras might provoke the dog owners into a new round of threats and abuse. We did as much of the installation inside the house as we could. It came in a kit with the cameras, mounts, and a computer monitor and screen. We installed the cameras and mounts on pieces of plywood inside the house, prior to mounting the plywood on our windows on the exterior. We were stressed and took deep breaths as we took the plywood pieces outside to install them, and fortunately, there was no incident with the neighbors.

All summer long, I felt as though I had been thrust into a primal protective mode, especially because Anne was incapacitated with her injuries. I often visualized myself sitting on the front steps of an Old West homestead, with a shotgun across my knees, desperately guarding my family against some lurking threat. The city authorities appeared to be doing nothing regarding either the dogs or their owners, so I felt all alone trying to protect Anne, our animals, and our home. It turns out the city authorities were doing a lot behind the scenes, but I did not know about it, so I felt abandoned by them until I later learned otherwise.

The dog owners effectively stole our back yard from us. Prior to the dog attack, we loved our yard and we spent many summer evenings working in our garden, grilling, drinking wine and listening to the live music that the Ramirez family played next door. The dog owners stole that from us with their threatening and abusive behavior, and we never went in the back yard except as necessary for the dogs to go out. We stopped taking our trash out through the back gate to the alley, and instead would take it out front, load it in the car, and drive it around to the alley or throw it in a dumpster in nearby Humboldt Park.

We developed a security ritual for taking our dogs out in back the back yard. Before we went out we would check to make sure we both had our pepper spray and cell phones. The pepper spray was a black canister with a belt clip, and a red tab to push down if I wanted to spray. It was advertised to spray up to 15 feet. I would clip the canister to my belt, and pull my shirt up over it to make sure it was visible to Lizzie and Wade. Then Anne would turn on her cell phone camera to record, so we would have an audio and visual record if there was any incident. We would then venture into the yard, on high alert, feeling like we were running a gauntlet. Anne had reams of footage on her cell phone of us taking the dogs out in the yard. Our dogs were very well behaved, as if they understood the gravity of the situation. They always did their pee and pooh very quickly, and rarely barked, which was uncharacteristic for them because both are hyped-up terrier mixes who usually bark a lot. Our dogs could sense our high level of fear and tension, and the threat from next door, and they modified their behavior accordingly. We always breathed a sigh of relief when we had taken the dogs out for the last time in the evening and were locked inside the house for the rest of the night.

We came home one day in August to find a note taped to the Lizzie's window, directly facing our house. It was hand written, in small enough letters that it was clear it was directed to us and was not meant to be read by passersby on the street. We could not read it because the letters were fairly small and partially obscured by glare and reflections from the glass. We could only read part of the first sentence, which began "*You know what you did. . .*" The rest of the note was illegible. We also did not want to lean over the fence and stare at it, since we feared that would provoke another incident. So, we were never able to read the entire note, but we were convinced it was meant for us, since there was no other reason for it to be there. Lizzie also put up several small round mirrors in her windows directly facing our house. We had no idea what this meant, but Anne speculated that Lizzie was implying that we were evil and the mirrors were meant to reflect our evil back at us.

Lizzie seemed to always be home, so we never got a reprieve from her verbal abuse or her creepily watching us. She had some type of clerical work from home job, so there was never a window of time where she was away at work. Not surprisingly, she also did not appear to have much of a social life, so she was basically always home.

We developed new nicknames for both Lizzie and Wade, "troll" for Lizzie and "monkey" for Wade. Lizzie earned the name because she seemed like an ugly troll, lurking under a bridge, waiting to spring out and terrorize unsuspecting passersby. We called Wade "monkey" because of his general ignorance and stupidity, and because his face a slight ape-like appearance.

Even when there was no incident, it was stressful because Lizzie was always obsessively watching us, which was creepy. When our friends helped us hack down the weeds, Anne and her friend Christine were loading the lawn care equipment into Christine's pickup truck. They caught Lizzie taking photographs of them through her front window. Christine waved at her, and Anne gave her a mock smile and thumbs up, and Lizzie retreated into the shadows of her house. We had no idea why she would want pictures of Anne and Christine loading stuff into a truck. Our best guess was that she wanted to use them in court to demonstrate that Anne was not that badly injured, since she was walking and moving stuff around, and that the dog attack was therefore not that severe.

There was a popular show on television called *"Orange is the New Black"* which was a drama set in a women's prison. Anne and I developed a running joke that we should call the producers of the show and sell them the rights to Lizzie's character. We had put up with so much shit from her, that we might as well make some money off her, we told ourselves. Her violent and bat-shit crazy personality, her creepy watching and notes, her lies and schemes to manipulate people, could make her one of the stars of the show.

We also decided that the best actress to play Lizzie would be Glenn Close, who played psychotic, dangerous female villains in the movies *"Fatal Attraction"* and *"Dangerous Liasons."* We joked about writing a script about Lizzie and sending it to Glenn Close's agent with an assurance that we had a role that was perfect for her.

Rosa told us of an incident where she caught Lizzie secretly watching her as she parked her car. She said she saw Lizzie's hand furtively pulling back her curtain to her front window which sent chills up her spine and felt like a scene in a creepy movie. Her description seemed perfect for a scene played by Glenn Close.

Ask me now if there were any preliminary warning signs about Lizzie and Wade and I would say yes, there was one. Prior to the attack, we learned of an incident which we should have detected as a red flag. Lizzie had told Anne about a traffic accident where she had a fender-bender in Chicago. The accident had occurred at a stop light. Lizzie had gotten out of her car, approached the other driver's car, and she reached through his front window and punched him in the face. She also said that she had a good attorney who had gotten her off. This was not any dirt we had later dug up on her. She had openly told Anne about the incident back when we still had a friendly relationship with her. I guess that was Lizzie's version of girl talk. She had told Anne, "I have to stop doing stuff like that." With the benefit of hindsight, this was a bright red flag indicating the true nature of Lizzie's character. But we did not pay much attention to it at the time, because we had a friendly relationship with her and Wade and were getting along well.

In retrospect, I do not believe that we ignored this red flag because we were naïve. We had lived in the Humboldt Park neighborhood of Chicago for 14 years, which had a tough reputation throughout the city. In addition Anne had taught for years in schools in the Austin and Englewood neighborhoods on the south and west sides of the city, the toughest neighborhoods in Chicago. I think we missed the warning signs from Lizzie because we did not know any violent or abusive people in our lives. The people in our social circles had their share of issues, but none of them could be considered violent or abusive. While we lived and worked in tough neighborhoods, we were not personally connected to any of the people involved in shootings, gang violence, or other criminal activity. So, we ignored the fact that Lizzie had punched a man after a traffic accident, something that with hindsight, we should have seen as a clear warning.

Thinking back about the prayer I had said with Lizzie and the hospital chaplain, it seemed like a surrealistic moment. Once I had learned Lizzie's true character, I was horrified that I had prayed with her and the hospital chaplain on the day of the attack. I felt like I had said a prayer with the devil!

I did not hate Lizzie and Wade because my hatred would be more of a compliment than they deserved. Hatred is reserved for people who mean something to you. A lover who has cruelly rejected you, an abusive or neglectful parent, a friend who has betrayed your trust, those are the people worth hating. Lizzie and Wade were worth nothing to me. Rather, they were dead to me. They simply did not exist as members of the human race. I viewed them with contempt and disgust as the two worst people we had ever met, but I refused to honor them with my hatred.

Of the two, we came to consider Lizzie to be the more dangerous. We certainly considered Wade to be a bad guy and were careful around him, but we felt that he was ultimately just an ignorant thug. Lizzie, however, was more intelligent than her husband, and was just smart enough to be completely bat shit crazy. As events escalated and became more strange and twisted, we became convinced that it was Lizzie who was driving the crazy train.

SHOULD WE STAY OR SHOULD WE GO

"You can contact that real estate agent all you want," I said to Anne. "But I'm not committing to moving at all. I'm not committing to anything!"

Anne was sitting at our dining room table looking at home listings on her lap top computer, with me looking over her shoulder. She had started to seriously consider moving, and a friend had referred her to a real estate agent who began to email her online listings. Anne started to show me houses she had looked at online, and I was willing to look at them, although I was a long way from agreeing that we should move.

"I'm just looking," Anne replied. "You don't have to commit to anything, just look at these listings and think about it."

I asked Anne what had motivated her to find a real estate agent, and she replied that it was that note that Lizzie taped to our mailbox. "That note really shook me up, it was very creepy!"

There were obviously many reasons to consider moving, and we had both mulled over the idea in our minds, but the note had tipped the scales in Anne's mind and prompted her to action. She began to proceed with preliminary inquiries. It had become clear that living next to Lizzie and Wade was an intolerable situation, which was making it impossible for us to begin healing and moving on from the dog attack.

At first, I strongly resisted the idea of the move. I hated that Lizzie and Wade were forcing us out of our neighborhood on their terms.

"I ain't gonna let these assholes make us move!" I thought to myself. *"We've been here for years longer than they have! If they don't like us they can move! They should have to move to a nice quiet neighborhood called the Illinois State Penitentiary!"*

On a practical level, I also knew that moving would be a huge job. Besides our normal household items, we had our artwork, equipment and art supplies, and boxes of stuff from my late parent's estate which we had yet to sift through. Moving would be very hard work under normal conditions and exponentially worse in our dangerous neighborhood situation.

But the stress of living next door to Lizzie and Wade had become excruciating, and my attitude toward moving began to shift. The decision was terribly difficult, because we had lived in the house for fourteen years, and had invested a tremendous amount of time, energy, and money into making it a home. Fourteen years was the longest I had ever lived in one place, even including my childhood home in Colorado.

We had bought the house in 1999 and it was a serious fixer-upper. Our early years living there were very difficult, because we could not afford to hire contractors, so we attempted to do as much work as possible ourselves. It was the first house we ever owned, and we were home improvement rookies, so we had no clue what we were doing. Both the kitchen and main bathroom needed major renovations, and there were plenty of other issues as well. We worked hard during the first few years we lived there, but seemed to get nothing accomplished.

"The Money Pit" is a funny movie comedy about a couple struggling to renovate an old house, and we often felt like we were living our own version of it. In one memorable scene, a bathtub crashes through the

floor of a second-floor bathroom, landing in the middle of the main floor living room, and the husband collapses into maniacal laughter.

The difference was that there was nothing funny about actually living that way. We became extremely frustrated with the lack of progress, which created serious tension between us, and we argued almost every day. It got so bad that in 2002 and 2003 Anne seriously considered moving out. The house was not only a money pit it was a black hole which consumed our time and energy as well as our money.

"If you want a divorce, buy a fixer-upper," our real estate agent had commented, and she was not kidding. It was amazing how much stress that house put on our relationship.

One of our worst arguments happened when my parents came to visit in 2001. They came to see the one-man art show I was having and to see our new home, which my mother was very excited about. At the time, they were in their late seventies and travel was becoming difficult for them. Their visit was very important to me because I knew that this could be the only time they ever saw a house that I owned, and I was right. Two years later, my father had a stroke and they did not travel after that. I was embarrassed and angry that I was showing them such a train wreck of a house, and Anne and I got into a huge argument on a Sunday morning while my parents were waiting for us at a restaurant where we were meeting them for brunch.

"I wanted to show my parents a home I'm proud of!" I yelled at Anne. "But this place looks like shit!"

"We're late to meet them for brunch!" I added angrily. "I'm gonna go meet them, you can stay here if you want, I don't care!"

"If you go without me, I'm leaving!" Anne screamed back. "And I don't mean just today, I mean I'm leaving for good!"

In the end, we resolved our argument and went to brunch together with my parents, and over the years, our living situation gradually improved. We taught ourselves to do a lot of home improvement work including installing copper pipes, sinks and toilets, PVC drain pipes, drywall, and cabinets. Anne became an expert in soldering copper pipe, better than most professional plumbers. I learned how to install tile, and I rebuilt and tiled a bathroom wall which looked great when it was finished. The kitchen was completely remodeled, and we did all the work ourselves except for the electrical wiring. We spent a lot of money hiring contractors to install a new fence, gutters and furnace. We had greatly improved the property from its original condition, and because we had invested so much time, energy, and money into our house, we were very conflicted about leaving.

One day however, something snapped in me and I realized that moving was the right decision. What changed my mind was a legal case pending regarding the identification of the attack dogs. Lizzie and Wade had concocted a lie saying that the dogs which had been seized by the police were not the same as the dogs that had attacked Anne. There was a court hearing scheduled to resolve this issue, and I realized that regardless of whether we won or lost, it would have a very negative impact on our home living situation. If we won and the dogs were banned from the city or euthanized, we would have to deal with the fury of Lizzie and Wade screaming threats and abuse at us and trying to get revenge any way they could. If they won and got their dogs back, we would have to endure them constantly parading the dogs in front of us, to rub in our faces their ugly little triumph, not to mention the danger of the dogs being back living next door to us. Regardless of whether we won or lost our legal case, it would still be a losing situation for us on the home front.

Another aspect which tipped the scales in my mind was a weekend in August when we house sat for a friend in a different neighborhood in Chicago. We were amazed by how relaxed we were once we were away from our stressful neighborhood situation. I went to bed about 6pm and slept like a baby because it was the first time in a couple of months that I had felt safe and secure. Once we were free from the neighborhood situation for a couple of days, we realized how emotionally debilitating it was, and made us understand that we needed to get out of that situation at all costs.

In August, we went to a family wedding in West Virginia, where Anne's cousin was getting married. West Virginia was the main base of Anne's extended family. Prior to the wedding, we went shopping for two new dresses, one for the wedding and one for the reception, as well as a new dress shirt and tie for me. This was emotional for Anne because it was the first time she had worn a formal dress since the attack, and she had tremendous anxiety about it. At the time the scars from her bite wounds were still very raw, a reddish color much darker than her natural skin. She worried about showing her shoulder scars, and she did not want to wear anything sleeveless. It was mid-August, so she had to find a light summer dress that would be comfortable in hot, humid weather. It was a dilemma for her to figure out what to wear. After an afternoon of shopping, she picked out two dresses, both in the same style, one blue and one black. They were both sleeveless, but she found a shawl in light fabric, blue background with white and yellow patterns. She draped this shawl over her shoulders at the wedding and reception to cover her scars.

We were concerned that Anne would not be able to go to the wedding. West Virginia is a twelve-hour drive from Chicago, and her doctors told her that sitting for such a long period could cause a risk of blood clots in her legs. Fortunately, the doctors approved her making the drive, with instructions that we stop every two hours for Anne to walk around, which would reduce the blood clot risk. Anne would have been extremely disappointed to miss the wedding, so we were thrilled with the doctor's decision. They had removed all of Anne's pinwheel drains except one, which was on the back of her right leg. She said later she was very conscious of it at the reception, because we were sitting on hard wooden chairs which pressed in on the drain.

The trip was just what the doctor ordered, because Anne's extended family is big and boisterous and knows how to throw a party. We had a great time at the wedding and reception, and it was a huge relief to cut loose and forget our troubles, if only temporarily. Anne was rejuvenated by spending a few days in the loving arms of her big family, and the trip was an important factor in making our decision that it was time to go.

At the reception, we had a productive conversation with Anne's uncle, who was a retired cop from the Los Angeles Police Department. We gave him the details of our neighborhood situation and told him we were considering moving but had not yet made a final decision.

"You should definitely move!" her ex-cop uncle advised us. "Move, get a good lawyer, and pound away on the dog owners from a distance!"

Our real estate agent, Jen, seized upon an opportunity for us to rent a condo while we looked for a house to buy and closed the sale. The condo was across the hallway from Jen's own condo and was available on a month to month basis because the owner had been unable to sell it. We loved the place, but it was expensive, and we worried about the cost.

"That condo is really expensive!" Anne said to me a couple of days before we made our final decision. "I don't think we should spend that much money on it! We should stay here until we close on a new house."

"I know it's expensive!" I replied. "I don't want to spend that much either. But we have to get out of here before something happens to us. It's dangerous!"

Ironically, our positions on moving had reversed 180 degrees at the eleventh hour before making the decision. I had become a strong advocate of moving into the rental condo immediately, while Anne had become averse to spending the extra money. I strongly lobbied to Anne that we simply could not continue to live next door to Lizzie and Wade and we would never be able to truly recover from the dog attack if we stayed there.

"Five years from now, we'll forget about spending this money," I argued to Anne, trying to convince her to take the rental condo. "But if we stay put and one of us gets hurt or killed, we will regret it for the rest of our lives!"

Ultimately, we both realized that while we did not want to take a financial hit, the money was not the most important issue. We simply had to get away from our awful neighborhood situation, whatever the costs or difficulties, and we made the decision to rent the condo beginning September 1st. We finalized the condo rental agreement on a Friday afternoon, and the following Sunday, we planned to meet with the owner to pay our deposit, get our keys, and begin moving in. Once the decision was made, the realization sunk in that this was the last weekend we would ever spend in our old home and a deep wave of sadness washed over me.

"I feel really sad!" I sobbed to Anne on the phone, having called her from work, standing alone in a storage vault. "This is going to be the last weekend we ever spend in our home, after 14 years!"

"I know baby. I know this is sad," Anne replied in a soft, soothing tone of voice, attempting to comfort me. "But this also gives us a chance at a new beginning! Please try to see that side of it."

I was in tears when I called Anne that Friday afternoon, realizing that this era in our life was ending. Despite our love-hate relationship with our house we were very emotionally attached to it because we had put so much time and hard work into renovating it. That house had been our home for 14 years, and we had done a lot of living under its roof. It was a very painful and difficult decision to walk away.

Besides missing our house, I knew I would miss the Humboldt Park neighborhood as well. Driving home from work that day, I noticed how rough the neighborhood looked. There were metal grates over every shop window, and tall black metal locked gates in front of every house, with graffiti everywhere. I never paid much attention to this during our years of living there, but now that we were leaving, it stood out to me.

Anne was raised in a quiet, pleasant suburb of Toledo, Ohio, and I was raised in small tourist and ski resort towns in the Colorado Rocky Mountains, both mostly white communities. Humboldt Park could not possibly be more different than the neighborhoods where either of us had grown up. Yet, in this gritty, multi-ethnic, urban neighborhood Anne and I had somehow found a home. Humboldt Park was always so alive it exuded so much energy that there was a tough beauty to it. That hard-edged neighborhood will always have a soft place in our hearts as our home of 14 years.

Although it was a hard decision for Anne as well, she seemed to be less conflicted about moving than I was. Maybe it was because she was the victim of the attack and was desperate to move away from the crime scene. Maybe it was because Anne is, in general, more adaptable and open to change than I am. Whatever the reasons, Anne was ready to go.

"I am going to miss our yard a lot." Anne said to me as she looked out our back window on our last Saturday afternoon in our house. It was the main feature we always loved about the Humboldt Park property. In character with us, it was unkempt and overgrown, but it was beautiful. Chives and mint grew wild. A peony flower bloomed about one week out of the year with full blossoms of pink and white petals. It was spectacular but short lived, like a fireworks display. Tall roses of varying colors which had been planted by Anne lined the fences, and we had two separate sections fenced off for garden vegetables. The roses grew so tall that the longest stems arched over the yard like a gateway. An eight foot wood stockade fence bordered the yard, giving us a lot of privacy, and we felt like it was our own private sanctuary.

Late Saturday night on our last night in our house, I sat out on our back steps looking out at our back yard. We had abandoned our back yard because of the threat from the Lizzie and Wade next door, and we never went out except to take our dogs out, to take trash out, and to do yard maintenance. We had forsaken the prior pleasures our yard provided us, like grilling, gardening, and sitting out on nice evenings. But that last Saturday evening, I decided to sit out on the back steps. I sat within a few feet of the back door, with the door open, in case there was any trouble from Lizzie and Wade. It was 1am and Anne and our dogs had gone to bed, and I went outside and sat out on the steps by myself.

It was a quiet August evening, warm, humid and hazy. Off in the distance, I could hear the typical Humboldt Park tapestry of urban background noise, traffic, people talking and shouting, and the occasional siren, car alarm, fireworks, and even gunshots. I was not thinking about Lizzie and Wade, and I was not sitting out as some act of defiance toward them. I simply wanted to enjoy our back yard on our last night living there after 14 years.

One of the most beautiful things about our back yard was that Anne had set up solar lights. These were all different colors and shapes, and some of them blinked or changed colors at various intervals. One was in the shape of a purple dragonfly, another a rose that changed colors from green to red, and there was a row of white lamps that we hung on the fence. Rarely were all the solar lights on at once, because it depended on their battery strength and the amount of sunlight that day.

But on our last night at our house, every solar light lit up the back yard, all at full strength. They were all shining brightly, blinking and changing colors through the August haze, in every corner of the yard. It was a beautiful light show, which illuminated our garden space, lawn, and flowers in a soft radiant glow. I enjoyed this beautiful solar light show which felt like it was meant for me as a final display, as if our yard, the place where we had put in so much work and spent so many wonderful hours, was bidding me farewell.

On September 1st we signed a one month lease for a condo in the Old Irving Park neighborhood of Chicago. We intended to rent this condo as a temporary residence to get us away from the awful situation with the dog owners, while looking for a house to buy. Since it was temporary, we wanted to move as few furnishings as possible into the condo, like kitchen essentials and toiletries. It was unfurnished, but we only moved in an air mattress and two folding chairs that we normally used for outdoor concerts and camping trips.

The condo was very nice, with hardwood floors stone counter tops, and a big picture window in the front that let in great natural light. Its best feature was access to a rooftop deck, on the fourth floor which provided a beautiful view all the way to the downtown skyline. It was across the hall from Jen's residence with whom we were becoming fast friends. During the process of finding our new house, Jen had kept up a professional demeanor appropriate to our business relationship. But as we got to know each other, we became friends with her and her partner Jim, who was a talented photographer. Jen was an olive-skinned woman with straight black hair who sometimes had to walk with a cane because she suffered from MS. Jim had white hair with a mustache and goatee. His favorite recreational activity was to ride his motorcycle, and he often wore Harley-Davidson t-shirts.

As our friendship grew, Jen let her hair down with us. She knew how to laugh, cut loose, and have a good time. She was passionate about holistic healing, raw and organic foods, and other aspects of healing and spiritual wellness. She gave Anne a protective crystal, which Anne carried in her purse everywhere she went. Jen's and Jim's condo was fascinating, filled with huge potted plants, incense burners, and unique and eclectic pictures and objects. One of my favorites was a framed Fleetwood Mac poster from a 1977 concert in Oakland, California.

Every evening, we met Jen and Jim on the deck to have a glass of wine, enjoy the view and the great September weather, which was the best weather of the year in Chicago. From the deck, we could see both of Chicago's tallest buildings, the Hancock and Willis towers, and a Ferris wheel set up on Navy Pier. Jen and Jim had set up the rooftop deck as their own space, with a grill, table and chairs, and numerous beautiful large potted plants which formed a garden that ringed the entire rooftop. Jen cooked several great meals for us, and we tried to return the favor as much as we were able, although we were so overwhelmed that we were unable to give back as much as we got.

The month living in the condo turned out to be a profound transformation for our lives. It was as though we were being reborn, and the feeling was exhilarating. We had fun with the bare bones living arrangements, where the two lawn chairs served as our couch, a box our coffee table, and an air mattress our bed. We felt like 20-something kids straight out of college who had just moved into our first apartment. We felt great that we had made the bold move to break free of the terrible situation in our old neighborhood, and we had made the first step into a new life. We were refugees in the sense that we were fleeing from a dangerous and excruciatingly stressful situation, but we were refugees living very comfortably, staying in a nice place, eating very well, and having a great time hanging out with our new friends on the rooftop deck. This month has developed a magical quality in our memory, as a time we were free from the burden of all our problems, free from the burden of our material belongings, and excited about exploring a new world and starting a new life.

THE MOVE FROM HELL

"I'm speechless!" our real estate attorney said on the phone after I had finished explaining our situation to him. "I'm speechless! I'm so sorry you are going through all this!"

I had decided to call him because we were pushing up against deadlines, and I realized that he did not know our background. To him, we were just another couple trying to buy a house, and he had no idea about our dire circumstances. During our month in the condo we found a house, made an offer which was accepted, and the wheels were turning on closing the sale. The house was a brick, bungalow style single family home in a nice neighborhood in Chicago, and we immediately fell in love with both the house and the neighborhood. But closing a sale on a house takes time and can get complicated, and, as the end of September approached, we grew worried that we would not close before our one-month condo lease expired. The sellers were starting to waver on making some repairs which were required as part of the sale agreement, and we were afraid this would delay or even cancel the closing.

If we did not close by September 30th we would be left with two bad choices. We would either need to pay another month's rent on the condo which we could not afford or move back into the old house next door to the evil neighbors until the closing was complete. For that reason, I had decided to call our real estate attorney and give him a basic overview of the dog attack and our war with Lizzie and Wade. He was shocked, and from that point forward he seemed to fully understand our desperation.

Fortunately, we had great support in finalizing the closing. Jen was our hero because she understood our urgency and was working hard to push through the fastest closing in real estate history. Her finance team was also desperately trying to get the mortgage loan approved as quickly as possible.

Our month in the condo had been a wonderful time, but as the deadlines loomed closer, the fun was tempered by the fact that we knew our real life was out there waiting for us, and we faced major challenges in our upcoming move. We had a lot of stuff to move, and we needed to complete unfinished remodeling projects to get the house ready to rent or sell. We would have to do this huge job under the dark lurking threat from Lizzie and Wade, running a gauntlet with every single load.

Despite some stressful last-minute glitches, we closed the sale on our new home on time, and were able to move out of the condo and into the new home starting October 1st. We had two top priorities of items we wanted to get out of the old house as soon as possible, our finished artwork and our furniture. We had some beautiful pieces of antique furniture which we inherited from my parents, who had been major antique collectors long before antiques became popular. The pieces included a beautiful wood hall tree which had come from a courthouse in Silverton, Colorado, and a dresser with a mirror in tarnished, beveled glass, which they had bought in New Orleans in the 1950's.

On Saturday October 5, we scheduled a move of our largest, heaviest, and most valuable items. Since I worked for a moving and storage company one of the perks of my job was that I was able to borrow a company truck for personal use. I had a truck and three friends from work lined up to help us move. The sky was grey and hazy that morning with a chance of thunderstorms all day, so we were worried about the weather disrupting our plans.

We told Meredith about our moving plans and she was worried.

"I think you should request additional police presence on your block for your moving day," Meredith advised us when we informed her of our plans. "I'm concerned that Lizzie and Wade could be emotionally set off by seeing a moving truck and a group of your friends moving a lot of large stuff. This could potentially provoke a violent incident."

"We think that's a really good idea," we replied, and I followed up by emailing Maureen from the alderman's office. After the meeting with Maureen, we had kept in touch with her and informed her of any new developments. I emailed her, requesting additional police presence for that Saturday. She forwarded my email to the district police commander who sent the following reply.

"Consider it done," read the email from the district police commander. Those three words were all he wrote, and I loved his email because it was concise and to the point. He had a quote from General Colin Powell in his email signature, which read, *"There is no secret to success. It is the result of preparation, hard work, and learning from failure."* His three-word reply had a no-nonsense, can-do marine quality to it, which I appreciated. *"Consider it done."*

"We know we're in a bad situation when we need to get a police escort for our moving day!" Anne and I said to each other. We found it extremely disturbing that we had to contact the police to notify them about our moving day, and that brought home to us how twisted our normal reality had become.

In addition, I was very worried about my friends' safety. I did not want to drag them into our dangerous neighborhood situation, and I would feel terrible if anything happened to place them in harm's way.

"Please feel free to say no," I said to each of our three friends I asked to help us move. "We'll be working next door to dangerous people! If you are not comfortable with that go ahead and say no, I understand." They all said they understood and were still willing to help.

The morning of the move, I arrived early at my work warehouse to pick up our truck. Before leaving, I cut two pieces of cardboard and taped them over the company name and logo on the doors of the truck.

"Why are you doing that?" my coworker Ben asked me. "You don't have to cover the logo when you borrow a company truck."

"I know," I replied. "I'm concealing it because I don't want the dog owners to know where I work. I don't want them coming after me at work!"

This exchange brought home to me what a creepy, alternative reality we were living in. I had to cover the company logo because we were living in a state of hyper-vigilance, which Ben or anyone living a normal life could not understand. I knew Lizzie and Wade could easily find the name and address of my workplace online, since my name and job title were on the company website. But I figured that if they wanted to track me down at my job, I should at least make them work at it, so I covered the logo on the truck.

I had specifically asked Ben to help because of his appearance. He was a large, powerful man, bald with tattoos on his arms including one of a tiger, and he bore a resemblance to Chicago Bears middle linebacker Brian Urlacher. Despite his appearance he was actually a thoughtful, intellectual artist, but he would be intimidating if you did not know him and saw him alone in a dark alley. I hoped that having this large, imposing, tattooed friend help us move would serve as a deterrent to Lizzie and Wade.

I drove the truck to our house with Ben and another friend, Andrew, while Anne drove our van to a Metra train stop to pick up a third friend, Jeanine. We got to the house before Anne and our front gate was locked, and I realized I did not have the key. Because we had switched vehicles, my gate key was on the van keys which were with Anne.

"Oh shit!" I said to Anne on the phone. "I don't have the front gate key!"

"I told you to remember to switch it!" Anne replied sharply, a tone of annoyance in her voice. We could not start moving because we could not get in the gate. I felt bad because Andrew and Ben were standing around wasting their time, and I was extremely worried that they were in full view of the front window of Lizzie and Wade, who were undoubtedly watching our every move. Fighting back panic, I frantically climbed over our back fence to get into our house to look for an extra gate key but could not find one. Fortunately Anne and Jeanine arrived quickly with the gate key, but it showed how the tension with Lizzie and Wade exacerbated even a minor snafu.

There was no incident with Lizzie and Wade, although Ben did catch Lizzie watching us through their front window, and he waved at her. We were very pleased that this part of the move came off without a problem, because we would have felt terrible if we had inadvertently dragged our friends into our neighborhood battle and placed them in any danger. Our friends worked very hard. It was an unseasonably hot and humid day in early October, feeling more like August, which made the physical work draining. All of us were drenched in sweat, and I had completely soaked through my shirt.

I worked with Andrew and Ben to load the truck full of art and furniture, while Anne and Jeanine worked together loading our own van with boxes. It was the first time Anne and Jeanine had met each other and I was hopeful they would get along well. My friendship with Jeanine had become a very meaningful source of support, and I would have been upset if she and Anne did not like each other. Fortunately they hit it off. They worked together all day and became a good team that worked well together and got a lot accomplished.

The police stopped by to talk to us as we were finishing loading. The officer was a blonde woman in her 30's, very nice and calm, exhibiting a positive energy. She parked her police car in the middle of the street directly in front of Lizzie and Wade's house and positioned herself where she could be clearly seen. She stood facing their front window, in a very forceful stance with her feet apart and her thumbs hooked inside her bullet proof vest.

"I've been driving down your block regularly keeping an eye on your house," she told us, also asking Anne, "How are the bite wounds healing?"

We really appreciated having the police and the alderman's office paying this kind of attention to us and our situation. Prior to the attack, the police paid little attention to our block because they did not need to. Anne and I were amazed and humbled that in a tough neighborhood in the third largest city in the nation, the police had changed their strategy specifically because of us, and we were very grateful. All of the police cars in Chicago have a sign on them saying *"We serve and protect."* We felt that was exactly what they did for us.

Afterward, we had a relaxing lunch we on our new back yard patio, enjoying pizza and beer after finishing unloading.

"Your new place is beautiful!" our friend Andrew remarked. Andrew was a 60 something working class black man who had lived his whole life in the Austin neighborhood on the west side of Chicago. I had worked with him for years, and he was a great guy with a keen sense of humor which always helped lighten the mood in our workplace. Although he was the oldest of us, he worked as hard as anyone in the hot, humid weather and, at one point, carried a large armchair out of the house by himself.

When we were finished with lunch, Anne gave our three friends rides home in our van, and I took the truck back to the warehouse. The rain began falling just as I finished returning the truck. It had held off just long enough to allow us to finish the job. Despite all our worries and stressful preparation leading up to our moving day, it went as well as we could have hoped. No news was good news in our situation, and we were very pleased and relieved that nothing had happened to our friends with Lizzie and Wade. I could not have written any better script for that day.

Although our moving day had been an excellent first step, a huge job still loomed in front of us. The move would have been a difficult job under the best of circumstances. But the difficulty was greatly compounded by another factor, which was that Lizzie and Wade gave us constant threats and harassment throughout the move, and every single load we carried out felt like running a gauntlet. Even when nothing happened, we were constantly on guard that something might, and that need for constant vigilance was exhausting. This unpredictability exacerbated the stress of the whole situation, because we did not know what might set off Lizzie and Wade. This was likely part of their strategy of intimidation, to keep us worried and on edge about what they might do. The relentless pressure, combined with our physical exhaustion, created major tensions between me and Anne, and we were often irritable and bickering with each other.

"I'm working like a fucking pack mule here!" I snapped at Anne as I angrily tossed a box of her yarn into our van. This was a line I came to say regularly as the move dragged on and our frustration continued to build. Anne grew to hate the "pack mule" line and it was guaranteed to either start an argument or exacerbate an existing argument every time I said it. As the move and renovations dragged on, seemingly endlessly, it became increasingly difficult to maintain a positive attitude.

"Shut up with all your pack mule bullshit!" Anne would snap back at me. "I'm so sick of hearing it!"

An incident occurred in October involving a group of Lizzie's friends. We were loading our van in front of our house, carrying boxes of books out, and a car pulled up in front of our house with four people in it. Apparently, they were Lizzie's friends because she immediately came outside and started talking to them, leaning in the car window while they sat in the car. We could not make out everything they were saying, but from what we could hear it was clear that they were talking about us. We heard Lizzie point out to them which cars were ours. They all were repeatedly gesturing and pointing toward us, our house and our vehicles, and their behavior made Anne and me fearful about what they were up to. Most disturbing of all was that Lizzie was laughing continually in a shrill, maniacal tone which was chilling to hear.

"I think you should come inside until these people leave!" Anne said to me. "We can work inside packing until they're gone!"

"I don't want to come inside!" I vehemently replied. "Our van's half loaded and I want to get it done. I'm sick of these fucking people! I'm not gonna let them disrupt our work!"

"Ok but I'm really worried!" Anne replied. "Should we call 911?! I think so!"

"What are we going to tell the cops?" I asked. "Yeah, these people seem creepy, but they can always tell the cops they're just having a conversation in front of their house. There's nothing illegal about that!" Lizzie and Wade seemed to understand the legal boundaries, because they were often able to act threatening and intimidating toward us but would stop short of giving us justification to call the police or file for an order of protection.

"I really don't want you going back out there!" Anne said as I picked up another box and pushed open the screen door. "But if you insist, I'm going to stand here and watch you with my phone out ready to call 911!"

I resumed carrying boxes out to our van while Anne stood in the front doorway, phone in hand. It was a beautiful sunny Saturday afternoon in October, and as I carried out loads, I passed within a few feet of Lizzie and her friends with each trip. We felt vulnerable because our front door and gate were open and the back hatch to our van was raised. I was afraid and my heart was pounding but I made every effort not to show it. With each trip back into the house, I walked slowly by their group with my hands in my pockets and a couple of times I smiled in Anne's direction as I passed, trying to send the message that I was not intimidated and was not scurrying in and out of our house like a frightened rabbit.

Lizzie continued to laugh very loudly as I made my trips in and out of the house, and it was obvious that she was pitching her laughter higher to make sure Anne and I heard it. The tone of her laughter was shrill and piercing, shrieking like a crazed banshee who was teetering on the edge of sanity, and it was chilling because it made us wonder what she was truly capable of. After about an hour, Lizzie's friends drove off and we never saw them again.

"What was the point of all that?!" Anne and I wondered after Lizzie's friends had left. Lizzie had gone back inside, we had finished loading and were driving home to our new house. There had been no incident to report to the police, no specific physical or verbal threats directed toward us from either Lizzie or her friends. Yet it seemed obvious that Lizzie had been playing some elaborate psychological game meant to intimidate us and instill fear and confusion. To that extent, she had succeeded, and we were worried about what she might be plotting with this weirdly sinister group of friends whom she had introduced into the picture. What lies had she told them about us?! Who where they, that they would agree to participate in her ugly little game?!

After the incident Anne described it to her mother, and they both thought I had been reckless and had put myself at risk. I did not view it that way. Rather, I was determined to continue with my work because it was a sunny fall afternoon and I was not going to let these creepy people interrupt me from getting the job done.

As the situation evolved, we developed a strict policy of not speaking to Lizzie and Wade or reacting to them in any way, other than to call the police if necessary. If there was any incident with them, we did not respond to them or even look in their direction, and we were extremely disciplined about adhering to this policy.

There were two reasons for this. We did not want them to goad us into escalating an incident that might become violent and we began to believe that in a dark and twisted way, Lizzie actually wanted a relationship with us, even if that relationship took the form of an ugly shouting match. She wanted some form of interaction with us. "*Feel free to ignore us in the future, as we will feel free to ignore you.*" Lizzie had written in the note she taped to our mailbox. We would have loved it if Lizzie had done what she wrote, but she could not seem to live up to her own words. She seemed to have developed a weird and extremely disturbing obsession with us, and Anne in particular.

We also had to decide about whether to sell the house or rent it. We preferred to sell and be completely free and clear to put this traumatic experience in the rear-view mirror. Unfortunately, Humboldt Park property values were terrible at the time, and we would have lost a lot of money selling the house at that time. We considered just taking the loss and selling to cut our ties once and for all, asking ourselves if our emotional recovery was ultimately more important than the money. But we decided that Lizzie and Wade had already done so much damage in our lives that we refused to allow them to force us into making a bad financial decision about the sale of our house. We decided to prepare it as a rental property, which involved getting aspects up to code and finishing ongoing renovations.

One afternoon in November, a woman approached me when she saw me moving boxes.

"Is your house available to rent?" she asked me.

"It will be," I replied. "It's not ready yet because we're still moving and fixing it up, but we will be renting it when it's finished.'

"My son is moving to Chicago from Florida next spring, and will be looking for a place to live," she explained. "He works as a sheriff in Florida and is moving to Chicago to work in the sheriff's department here. Would you be interested in renting your house to him?"

"Hell yes, I'd be interested!" I exclaimed to myself. *"Are you kidding me, this guy's a goddamned sheriff! That's exactly what we need, a sheriff living next door to Lizzie and Wade!"*

"Yes, I would be interested," I replied with measured tones, trying to restrain my enthusiasm from bubbling over in too obvious a manner. "Let's exchange contact information and we can call each other in March or April to arrange a showing of the house."

"Oh my God! That would be great!" Anne exclaimed excitedly when I called her to tell her about the prospect. It would be the ultimate poetic justice to install a law enforcement officer next door to our violent, criminal neighbors. As I was leaving for the day, Arturo Ramirez drove by and stopped to talk. I told him that we had an opportunity to rent our house to a sheriff and he replied, "This block needs a sheriff!" Nodding in the direction of Wade's house Arturo balled his hand in a fist and made a punching gesture saying, "I'd like to kick his ass!"

In November, I had an annual checkup with my cardiologist. I had a heart condition called mitral valve prolapse which was benign but needed to be monitored by a cardiologist once a year. During the appointment, I was told I had high blood pressure.

"I have never had high blood pressure before," I told my cardiologist. "It's always been normal or somewhat low. Do you think stress could be the cause of it?"

I went on to explain our situation to him, and he replied that yes it could be the cause. He wrote on my checkout form that I was diagnosed with hypertension. I also lost 10 pounds during the move, although I was not trying to lose weight and was eating like a horse. I was 50 years old during the move, and it was the first and only time in my life I was ever diagnosed with high blood pressure.

Our work continued into the winter, and that winter was the worst Chicago had experienced in 30 years. Records were set for both snowfall and freezing cold temperatures. Chicago schools cancelled classes for the first time in 12 years because of dangerously cold temperatures.

"It's just my luck that we get record snowfall amounts during the year I have two houses to shovel snow at!" I remarked to Anne. Besides shoveling, I also had to check the Humboldt Park house regularly for frozen pipes, turning on every faucet trying to keep them from freezing. Our former home stood empty, bleak and desolate in the bitter cold. Slate grey light glinted off hardwood floors grimy from the snow salt we tracked in. Our voices and footsteps started to echo in the rooms as we gradually emptied them out. The harsh, brutal winter seemed to symbolize the state of our lives.

I developed a routine where I would stop by the house on my lunch break at work, and I would always text Anne when I got into the house and text her again after I left.

"No troll or monkey sighting," I would text Anne if I made it to and from the house without incident. We regularly used our nicknames for Lizzie and Wade in our texts. I adjusted my lunch break at work from around noon to later in the afternoon, around 2:00-2:30pm. The reason was that the elementary school across the street let out at that time. The street was packed with cars full of parents waiting to pick up their children, and parents walking home from school with their children. This made me feel safe because Lizzie and Wade would be deterred from attacking me with all these people out, and even if they did attack me there would be hundreds of potential witnesses.

Every time I made the turn onto our old block, I felt a terrible tension settle into my body. I felt the muscles of my jaw tighten as I approached the house, and my shoulders hunched up toward my neck. I carried pepper spray every trip I made to the old house. As soon as I turned the corner onto that block, I checked to make sure I had my pepper spray ready. Its canister had a clip where I could attach it to my belt, and then I would pull my shirt and coat up over it to make sure it was visible, so that Lizzie and Wade could see that I was carrying it.

I began to listen to a Bob Dylan song *"Mississippi"* whenever I was driving to the old house. It seemed to put me in the right frame of mind to deal with our situation, because it had edgy lyrics written from the perspective of a man who gets into some unspecified trouble in Mississippi.

"My clothes are wet, tight on my skin, but not as tight as the corner that I painted myself in. The only thing that I did wrong was stay in Mississippi a day too long."

Besides *"Mississippi"* another song I listened to regularly was *"Across the Border"*. This song was a great collaboration of musical legends, written by Bruce Springsteen, sung beautifully by Emmy Lou Harris and Linda Ronstadt, with some sweet backup harmonica work by Neil Young. It really spoke to me because our move was a monumental, desperate effort to cross a border into a new life, and escape from all the hardship of the old. One particular line seemed written for me and Anne: *"And in your arms 'neath open skies, I'll kiss the sorrow from your eyes, somewhere across the border."*

One day, Anne went over to the house by herself, which we normally did not like her to do, but we thought it would be ok because there were contractors working inside, remodeling our bathroom. Anne and I agreed that she would leave at the same time the contractors left, so she would not be at risk being left-alone at the house. Anne did leave at the same time as the contractors, but she thought she had forgotten to set the alarm, so she went back in, while the contractors got in their van and drove away.

Lizzie saw that Anne was leaving the house alone, and she seized on her opportunity and pounced!

"I know where you live, dog killer!" she screamed as Anne was locking our front door and leaving. "I'll follow you!"

Clearly, Lizzie had been watching every move that Anne and the contractors made, waiting for her chance to attack. It was eerie to know that Anne was being monitored so closely. Anne was only alone for a couple of minutes, but that was enough to give Lizzie an opening. I was upset with Anne for creating that window of risk, and I chided her, saying, "When I said leave with the contractors, I meant leave with the contractors, not leave five minutes after them! You put yourself in danger!"

Under normal conditions, we would have gone through all our stuff prior to the move, to organize what to throw out, donate, sell or keep. But because we felt so threatened being at the old house and the excruciating stress of that threat, we just wanted to get everything out, and we moved everything with absolutely no preliminary organization or packing. Plus, we felt vulnerable going out in the back alley, so we moved a lot of stuff that was basically trash. Many times, I loaded up our van with trash bags and moved them to throw out in the dumpsters in nearby Humboldt Park, and sometimes I even inadvertently moved bags of trash to our new house.

By March, we had moved out most items of value, and we had hired a company called 1-800-GOT-JUNK to remove an old sofa, a metal cabinet, chunks of drywall trash and broken cast iron pipe left over from our remodeling projects. It was a raw, grey Saturday morning and the 800-JUNK crew pulled their truck into the alley near Lizzie and Wade's garage door and Wade came out and started yelling at them that they were in the way. The junk truck was not in Wade's way, and even if it was, he could have just nicely asked them to move it, but of course he had to make a scene.

"I'm sick of this shit!" Wade yelled at the 800-JUNK crew, which made no sense because he and Lizzie were the source of all the problems on our block. Anne and I were fed up with them harassing people who were trying to work for us, so we decided to call the police.

"Hey, did somebody here call the police?!" a young African American man asked as he strode into our living room, wearing a shit-eating grin and a light blue work shirt which read 1-800-GOT-JUNK. "The police are out front!"

"Yeah, that would be us!" Anne and I replied raising our hands, with a wry smile on our faces.

"There's bad blood between these neighbors!" The police officer explained to a second cop who showed up after we had finished explaining the situation to the first officer. The officer had black hair combed straight back. He came into our house and looked all around our property inside and out, clearly trying to gauge what was going on in this situation.

"What is that?" He asked when he noticed a note which Lizzie had taped to her front window facing our house. "Is that for you?"

"We think so," we replied. "It's been there for months but we can't be sure because we've never been able to read it. The writing's too small and we're afraid it will provoke an incident if we get too close to try to read it."

The officer leaned as far as he could over our stair railing, peering at the note trying to read it. With him present we finally felt safe enough to get closer, so Anne and I leaned forward with him, the three of us straining to read the note.

"You know what you did!" read the first line, but none of us could make out the rest of the note because it was obscured by glare from the glass. But the first line made it clear that the note was for us and that Lizzie was accusing us of something.

"Man, those people are hillbillies!" exclaimed the second member of the 800-JUNK crew, who was much older than the first man, also African American. "They're dangerous!"

Anne and I proceeded to give him a summary overview of the situation, including the dog attack, Lizzie getting arrested after the police chase, and our lawsuit.

"Man, they must really hate your guts!" he said after we finished explaining the status of our lawsuit.

"Yeah, it's kind of like that!" we replied, shrugging our shoulders.

"Nobody can say we don't know how to throw a party!" I said to Anne after the 800-JUNK crew had finished loading their truck and left. We had quite the gathering that morning, with the 800-JUNK crew, plumbing and drywall contractors, Anne and me, Lizzie and Wade, and the police all in the mix at the same time. Lizzie had been harassing our drywall contractors by asking them continually if they had permits for their work. One of our contractors nodded in Lizzie's direction and made the gesture with his finger making a circle around his ear – crazy!

"At least we gave the 800-JUNK guys something to talk about when they get back to their warehouse!" Anne replied laughing.

"We had to call the police on Lizzie and Wade this weekend!" I told Jeanine the following Monday morning at work.

"Oh no!" Jeanine exclaimed, tossing her hair back and laughing. "What did she do this time?!"

"I know, I know!" I said. "Another day another 911 call!"

"What did you do this weekend?" I continued in a mock water cooler conversation. "Oh, just the usual, went grocery shopping, cleaned the house called the police on our neighbors, same old same old..."

One would think that I would have been offended that Jeanine thought it was funny that I called 911, but I laughed right along with her and was not offended in the least. I completely understood why she thought it was funny. Anne and I had developed a running joke that we should call the Chicago Police Department and ask if they offered a volume discount. Something like if you called 911 nine times you got the tenth call free. A Costco preferred customer executive membership card for the Chicago Police Department. Maybe you didn't even need to call 911; you could just swipe your card.

Although Lizzie remained dangerous and psychotic to us, we also found her to be darkly comic. Her antics were so ridiculous that they were funny in a very grim sort of way. She had evolved into a type of scary, creepy clown. We certainly continued to take her seriously as a threat, and never for a moment let our guard down, but increasingly we began to find humor in her behavior. The entire situation had disintegrated into a dark theatre of the absurd.

In May, the sheriff did move to Chicago, and we showed our house to him and his family. They were a Puerto Rican family, and the sheriff had a beautiful wife and two cute kids. They loved the house when we showed it to them. The wife loved the yard, and one of the little boys had already picked out his room upstairs.

"You can go home and talk about it amongst yourselves," we offered to them. "You can call us tomorrow with a decision."

"We don't have to talk about it," The sheriff replied. "We want the place!"

Anne and I were ecstatic! Not only had we found renters, we had found a law enforcement officer who would derail Lizzie and Wade's abuse train once and for all! We laughed visualizing the expression on Lizzie's face while she was creepily watching out her window seeing for the first time the sheriff leaving for work in the morning in his uniform. Once he signed the lease, with a stroke of the pen, Lizzie and Wade's reign of terror over our block would be over!

Unfortunately, the deal with the sheriff fell through at the last minute. He ran into some unexpected money problems and had to pull out right before he signed the lease. Anne and I were very disappointed and upset with him because we had held the house for him for a month when we could have been showing it to other prospective tenants.

Anne and I went to the house to pull weeds on a hot, bright Sunday morning in July. At long last, the move and remodeling work were finished, and all we had to do was mow the lawn and clean up the yard to have the place ready to show prospective tenants.

"It's about time!" Lizzie called down to us, rushing out on her tall balcony while we were pulling weeds.

"Doesn't she have anything better to do than to watch us?!" I muttered to Anne. "It's pathetic!"

"Maybe we should buy her a television," Anne replied. "Get her a subscription to Netflix so she'd have something to watch other than us!"

Lizzie went on to say something about how Anne and I did not talk to her and Wade any more. We could not hear her very well and could not understand part of what she was saying, but it made no sense to us. Why would she want us to talk to her and Wade since they obviously hated our guts? Her dogs had almost killed Anne, she had subjected us to constant threats and harassment, and she had lied under oath in the dog ID hearing. Did she expect us to invite her over for tea after all that?!

I turned and smiled toward Anne who was standing on our back steps. As the situation evolved, I increasingly found myself bluffing and posturing in Lizzie's presence. I would often smile or laugh when she was watching us.

"It's fucking hilarious isn't it?!" Lizzie shouted angrily. She whirled around and stomped angrily inside, slamming her sliding glass door behind her. As she left, she screamed back over her shoulder, "I place a curse on you and your house forever!"

It was in that moment that Anne and I knew we had won the war. We knew then that our rigorous policy of ignoring Lizzie and Wade had been the right approach. It had been very difficult to adhere to this policy and there were many times when we had to hold ourselves back to keep from engaging.

"You're an ignorant white trash cunt who belongs in prison! I wish those dogs would chew YOU up!" I imagined myself yelling at Lizzie many times. Normally, I would find it offensive to call a woman the c-word, but Lizzie was a special case and I made an exception for her. But no matter what we felt like to saying to Lizzie, our discipline never wavered, and we never said anything to her.

In that moment, Lizzie let her guard down and showed us that our ignoring her was getting to her, upsetting her more than anything we could have yelled back at her. In a twisted sort of way, Lizzie desperately wanted some sort of relationship with us. She also seemed to have a warped idea that somehow, we had victimized her, that we were the cause of her troubles, rather than her own actions and her vicious dogs. We had often thought that she felt very guilty about the dog attack, but that guilt was deeply buried to where she did not even realize it. She would never admit that guilt to herself and certainly not to anyone else, least of all Anne and me, so it manifested as angry verbal attacks on us.

After the rental deal with the sheriff fell through, we listed our house on a real estate website called Zillow. The response we got was overwhelming and we received more interest than we could handle. We selected several that sounded the best and made appointments throughout the day on a Saturday.

Of course, we were worried that Lizzie and Wade would try to disrupt our showings but happily, there was no incident. We asked ourselves if we had any moral, ethical, or legal responsibility to warn people that they would be moving in next door to horrible neighbors, and if so, what type of warning should we give them. After much discussion, we decided we should give people a generalized warning, without going into details about the dog attack or our history with the Lizzie and Wade.

"All the neighbors on the block are nice, except the white couple on the east side of you, those people are assholes," we advised our tenants when we first showed them the place. "Nobody on the block likes them, just stay away from them. The Mexican family on your west side is a great family, make friends with them."

"We should have done all this work while we still lived here," Anne and I said to each other. "This place looks great!"

Certainly, the reason for the high level of rental interest was that the place looked fantastic when all the remodeling was complete. The people we showed it to included three young art students who attended the Art Institute of Chicago. Being artists ourselves, we wanted to give these kids a chance, but we worried we were making a mistake and we had another interested married couple who was older with better credit. What tipped the scales was that two of the artist kids' fathers offered to co-sign the lease and pay the rent if the kids defaulted. We decided to rent our house to the three young artists and they signed the lease and began moving in on August 1st.

The move and renovations had taken ten long grueling months of hard physical labor and terrible emotional fear, stress and anxiety. It was the toughest job Anne and I had ever done, and it pushed us to the brink of a physical and mental breakdown. Looking back, I honestly do not know how we survived it. To call it the move from hell was not an exaggeration. When the young artists signed the lease on August 1st, we could not believe that the move from hell was finally over.

MISTAKEN IDENTITY

"Take all the time you need, Sweetie," I said to Anne, putting my hand on her trembling shoulder in an attempt to calm her down. "We can go back in when you're ready."

We were standing in a hallway just outside the Chicago Animal Control pound, and Anne was crying, her entire body shaking with fear. We were with Meredith, Anne's friend Christine, and Officer Johnson from Animal Control who had asked us to come into the pound to identify the attack dogs. Anne had tried twice to enter the pound but both times had a panic attack and was forced to retreat to the hallway outside to regain her composure. The hallway had white cinder block walls and a plexi-glass window which revealed the pound filled with cages containing many dogs of a wide variety of breeds. Besides the trauma of Anne having to see the attack dogs, the pound was also a deafening cacophony of dogs barking and yelping which increased her sense of panic.

"I'm ready," Anne said, taking a deep breath and exhaling sharply. Officer Johnson opened the door and the group of us went back inside the pound to see the attack dogs. Anne still trembled, but on this third try was able to keep her composure, and she positively identified both dogs that had attacked her. I was also asked to identify the two dogs. I studied both and remembered the distinctive grey and brown brindle coats, and white markings on their muzzles. What really made me sure was a distinctive gesture from the oldest, largest dog. When we stood in front of his pen to identify him, he leaped and lunged up to his right, slamming his paws against the side of his cage, just as he used to slam his paws against our fence when he was out front in their yard. It was the exact same gesture, and I had no doubt that he was the same dog, the pack leader, who had led the attack on Anne. This dog had always been extremely focused on me when he leaped against the fence of our property. We stood in front of his pen with several people, and the dog was staring straight at me as he lunged. It seemed as if he recognized me and knew I was the enemy, that he held me responsible for putting him in that cage. Both of us signed affidavits that we had identified the dogs as the same dogs that attacked Anne.

After we visited Animal Control to identify the dogs, a court hearing was scheduled regarding their identification. Meredith told us that Lizzie and Wade were working with an animal charity organization called the Buddy Project, which specialized in rescuing vicious dogs who were impounded and scheduled for euthanasia. The Buddy Project was named after a Rottweiler with that name, which had killed a smaller dog in a park. According to this charity, Buddy had been falsely accused of being a vicious dog and had been impounded and euthanized. The Buddy Project was assisting Lizzie and Wade with legal help to free their dogs who they claimed were falsely accused and were on "death row." The accomplishments of the Buddy Project included saving a pit bull which had killed a small child in Nevada. We found it disgusting that with so many worthy charitable causes in the world, the mission of the Buddy Project was helping dangerous people keep their vicious dogs.

Meredith also informed us that Lizzie and Wade had concocted a twisted, ridiculous lie about the identification of the dogs. They claimed that the dogs which attacked Anne had been removed to a dog shelter in South Dakota, where they were euthanized, and their remains were fed to coyotes, which was said to be standard procedure in that state. Then they had adopted two new dogs in Wisconsin, which were the dogs seized and impounded by Animal Control, and were completely different dogs from the ones that attacked Anne. The microchip identification implants had been transferred to the new dogs, which would explain how the microchips read them as being the original attack dogs. However absurd this story was, the judge decided to hear it, and we were ordered to attend a court hearing regarding the identification of the dogs.

I had a tennis match scheduled one Sunday morning, and my opponent made a mistake on his calendar and forgot about our match. I called Anne from the tennis court and said, "I figured out why my tennis partner never showed up. He was sent to South Dakota and his remains were fed to coyotes!" "It wasn't really him," Anne replied. "It was his evil twin micro chipped as him!" This was just one of many jokes both us and our attorneys had about the case. We all thought that Lizzie and Wade's lie was absurd, and we were confident that it had no chance of winning in court. Anne called the head partner of our law firm to ask about it, and he scoffed in his reply saying, "They're not getting those dogs back!"

The hearing was held at a courthouse in a neighborhood near downtown Chicago known as River North, a couple of blocks from Chicago's main art gallery district. The courthouse was a large square brick building that filled a whole city block, and it seemed to have no character whatsoever. Chicago is a city filled with architectural masterpieces in a wide variety of styles, but this building was not one of them. It appeared to be a new building, clearly built strictly for function, with no attempt whatsoever at aesthetics. The tall black tower of the John Hancock building dominated the background skyline.

It was a hot, humid August afternoon with bright sunlight, and Anne and I were sweating as we walked from our car to the courthouse. We had been forced to park a few blocks away, and we were both wearing formal clothes for the court hearing. Anne was scheduled as a potential witness to testify, and she was wearing a dark blue business jacket and skirt, against which her bright red hair stood out in the strong summer sunlight. I was wearing a black suit with a grey shirt and burgundy tie, and my long black hair was combed back and tightly braided.

The cool, artificial air conditioning was welcome as we entered the courthouse, and it immediately began to dry the sweat on our faces. We entered through the typical metal detector security. Anne sent her purse through on a conveyer belt, and I removed my belt, wallet, phone and keys to send them through as well in a plastic bin. Security guards wearing light blue shirts with badges oversaw the process.

"I don't want Lizzie and Wade to see you arriving!" Meredith said as she hastily ushered us into an empty hearing room off the main hallway. "I think it's too late," Anne replied. "I think Lizzie saw us when we first went through security." She had wanted to keep us physically separated from Lizzie and Wade because of the volatile situation between us and did not want them to see us entering the hearing because of their potential reaction. Unfortunately, Lizzie had been sitting on a bench near the entrance in a linoleum tiled cinder block hallway, and we were pretty sure she had seen us as soon as we walked in. "Just wait in here until the hearing starts," Meredith directed us.

We spent the entire hearing sitting on a bench in a hallway outside the hearing room, and we never went in to the hearing itself. There was a possibility that one or both of us could be called as witnesses, and therefore we could not attend the rest of the hearing. Meredith came out roughly every 30 minutes to give us updates on the proceedings. She told us we had won, largely because of a mistake that Lizzie and Wade had made. Before the attack, they had posted a photograph on their Facebook page of the dogs sitting on their front porch looking out toward the elementary school down the street. When they tried to create the scam that the new dogs were different dogs, they accidentally posted the same photograph again on their Facebook page, this time labeled as being the "new" dogs, with different names. This piece of evidence was displayed at the hearing, and it was proof that Lizzie and Wade were lying about the identification of the dogs.

After the hearing was over, we saw Lizzie sitting on the floor at the other end of the hallway. She was crying, sitting with her back against the wall and her legs straight out like an angry child, with both Wade and her attorney consoling her. We left the hearing very happy and relieved that the dangerous dogs were finally and officially removed for good.

One Saturday morning about a month later, I found Anne crying as she walked up are basement stairs.

"Why are you crying, Sweetie?" I asked Anne in surprise, "What's wrong?!"

Anne had been in a pretty good mood, so I had no idea why she was suddenly so upset. We had a maintenance man working on our furnace in the basement, and my first thought was that he had done something rude to Anne but that was not the problem.

"Meredith just called me," Anne replied, her voice quaking. "The judge decided to reopen the dog ID case."

"What the hell?!" I exclaimed. "I thought she told us it was a done deal?!"

"What happened?!" we asked Meredith when we called her back, putting her on speaker phone so we both could hear her.

"Lizzie and Wade found some new witnesses from Wisconsin who were willing to lie for them," She answered. "This was enough to convince the judge to reopen the case." We were very surprised and upset because we had been told that the dog identification case had been closed, and that there was no way Lizzie and Wade were getting the dogs back. We were amazed that such an absurd, convoluted lie was being seriously considered in a court of law for the second time, but it was, and we were ordered to attend the second hearing.

Our understanding was that the City of Chicago was negotiating with Lizzie and Wade about what to do with the dogs, but that they would never be returned to them. We were also informed that Anne had been ordered to testify at the second hearing and face cross-examination from the dog owners' attorney. Anne's previous testimony and identification of the dogs had been traumatizing for her, and for her to have to do it again only made it worse.

Later in the day, after we received the bad news, I took our dogs Alice and Pandora for a walk in a nearby park. This turned out to be a bad idea because I was too upset to have any patience handling them. Alice kept pulling on her leash lunging at squirrels in the park and I got extremely frustrated with her.

"Quit lunging at those goddamned squirrels!" I angrily yelled at Alice, yanking her leash back so hard that her paws came off the ground. A couple of old ladies sitting on a nearby park bench shot me a dirty look and I felt bad because I realized that to them I looked like an abusive dog owner. I yanked Alice's leash back too hard because I hated seeing her lunge at squirrels. I was acutely aware that Alice wanted to do the same thing to the squirrel that the attack dogs had done to Anne. I had started to dislike her and Pandora, even though they were small terrier mixes who loved me and Anne. Any aggressive behavior from them reminded me that dogs are predatory animals, which in turn reminded me of what had happened to Anne. Luckily, Alice was not hurt and when we got home I gave her an extra dog treat as an apology.

The second hearing was scheduled for Friday October 18th. Upon arrival at the courthouse, Meredith ushered us into a small windowless white cinder block room adjacent to the main courtroom, where we were to spend most of the day. Initially, I had gotten separated from everyone else in our party, and I did not know where the rest of them went. I walked into the courtroom and the only people present were Lizzie and Wade, their friends, and their attorneys. I sat awkwardly on a wooden bench for a few minutes on the other side of the room, not knowing where my people were, alone in the courtroom with our enemies. Pretty soon Meredith came and found me and escorted me into the side room where we stayed throughout the hearing.

Before the hearing began, I excused myself to go to the restroom. As I walked down the hallway to the restroom, I saw Lizzie and Wade standing in the middle of the hallway with their attorney and friends, talking in a circle. When I passed them, I walked straight through the middle of their circle. I wanted to send them a message, *"I'm here, I'm not going anywhere you are present at this hearing because of me."* Although I was safe because of courtroom security, I still felt threatened by Lizzie and Wade. I was alone in the men's restroom and

I worried that Wade would come in and confront me there.

Attending the hearing were Meredith, Officer Johnson and one of his colleagues from Animal Control, and an attorney representing the City of Chicago. Also present were two women who managed a dog rescue organization from which the attack dogs had originally been adopted out. Anne, the animal control officers, and the dog rescue owners were all scheduled to give testimony. The dog rescue owners went first, and they positively identified the dogs as the same dogs they had adopted out to Lizzie and Wade. One of them testified that the Lizzie had both bribed and threatened her to give testimony about the dogs. She said that Lizzie had come to her after the attack and told her, "I need you to lie for me." She refused to do so, and then Lizzie started attacking her dog rescue operation, accusing them of financial mismanagement and tax evasion.

The dog rescue owner was a small white woman, probably less than 5 feet tall, and she expressed genuine remorse that she had adopted the dogs out to Lizzie and Wade. She openly admitted that she had been played by Lizzie, saying that she thought Lizzie was a nice person. She initially had reservations about Wade, but he had interacted well with the dogs when they had visited. She felt that the dogs had an issue with men because of some previous abuse, but they seemed to like Wade, so she agreed to adopt them out.

"The dogs were found tied to a telephone pole in Gary Indiana," The rescue owner explained to us giving background history of the dogs. "Someone tied them to the pole and just left them when they were puppies. They were abandoned!" The dog rescue organization found them and sheltered them until they were later adopted by Lizzie and Wade.

So, the dogs never had a chance to be normal dogs that would interact with people or other animals in a positive way. After a history of abuse and neglect, they had been adopted by violent criminals. Given their background, it was no wonder that they turned out to be vicious monsters which would attack Anne the moment she opened their front door. It was not their fault that they were vicious monsters. They were monsters that human beings had created.

"I believe Lizzie really does love those dogs," Anne and I said to the rescue owner. "The problem is that it's not a healthy kind of love. It's a love that's dark, twisted, and obsessive, a love which completely blinds her to how dangerous her animals are!" The dog rescue owner agreed, and said she requested a security escort to take her out to her car after her testimony, because of the threats and coercion she had received from Lizzie.

The next person to testify was Officer Johnson from Animal Control. He was attending with his assistant, a younger Latina woman. She was not a witness and was not required to be there, but she had wanted to attend the hearing because she was angry about the case and wanted to see what happened. It was actually her day off, but she still attended the hearing because she felt so strongly about it. She said that she and other staff had been verbally abused by Lizzie during regular visits she made to Animal Control to see the dogs.

In one instance, the Animal Control manager had to threaten to call 911 to make Lizzie leave. "Nine!" the manager had shouted, phone in hand looking Lizzie straight in the eye. "One!" She said dialing the second number. "One! Last chance to leave or I'm calling!" she said with her finger on the third number, and just as she was dialing, Lizzie stormed out of Animal Control screaming a torrent of threats and insults in her wake.

After Officer Johnson was finished, Anne was called to testify. She had been dreading this moment since she first got the phone call that she had been called as a witness. Anne was visibly shaken, her hands trembling. Meredith gave her some last-minute advice and I put my arm around Anne as she was doing so, and then we were ushered into the hearing room.

Once Anne actually took the witness stand she did very well in answering the questions and maintained her composure beautifully. The attorney for Lizzie and Wade showed Anne a series of photographs of dogs, asking her to answer yes or no as to whether they were the dogs that attacked her. He tried to trip her up by showing her photographs of dogs that looked similar to the attack dogs but were not them. He even showed two photographs of dogs from the rescue where Meredith volunteered, attempting to confuse Anne. Their attorney had a sleazy persona, with slicked back, dark hair, highly polished shoes, and a cheap looking suit. His demeanor reminded me of the sleazy attorney on the television show *"Breaking Bad"*. Better call Saul! At one point he went over the line when he asked Anne to describe the details of the attack, asking if one of the dogs had dragged her down the stairs by her buttock. The judge intervened and stopped that line of questioning.

The judge gave me a bad feeling from the moment we walked into the hearing room. He was an older white man who looked well into his 60s and possibly over 70. He had white hair and he glared out into the courtroom from under bushy, white eyebrows. If he had long hair and a beard he could have been cast as a wizard in *"Lord of the Rings."* I saw him several times staring straight at me, seemingly asking himself who the hell I was and why I was in his courtroom.

Legally, the case was between the City of Chicago versus Lizzie and Wade, not us versus them. For that reason, it was not Meredith but the City of Chicago attorney who represented our side of the case. The judge spoke very gruffly in a gravelly voice to both attorneys and seemed to be especially rude to the City of Chicago attorney. He was a very young man who looked to be under 30. He was small in stature, with blond hair and a neatly trimmed beard. He seemed very nice and he tried to make us comfortable and at ease as much as possible under the circumstances, even bringing us chairs in the waiting room. But as the testimony progressed, it became apparent that he was too weak and inexperienced to represent our side of the case effectively. His follow up questions were unclear and indecisive, and he seemed intimidated whenever the judge confronted him with a question. By contrast, Lizzie and Wade's attorney seemed like a shark. Since the judge was gruff and intimidating, we started to worry that the City attorney was in over his head.

Other than Anne, I did not watch most of the testimony. I was not allowed to because I was a potential witness, and witnesses were not permitted to watch the testimony. About half way through the proceeding, I was told that I would not have to testify, which meant that I could watch the rest of the proceeding.

Lizzie was scheduled to testify next, and I went into the hearing room and picked a spot on a wood bench in front, in full view of her, with Meredith sitting next to me. I wanted her to see me with our attorney, to be physically as close to her as possible, because I was hoping my presence would make her lose her composure. I do not know if I succeeded in rattling her, but her performance on the witness stand was terrible. She often seemed flustered and confused, and regularly interrupted her testimony with nervous laughter. Her testimony itself was ridiculous. Her explanation for the confusion about the "new" dogs was that she had a disagreement with Wade about naming them. She said that she liked the original names for the dogs, but Wade had wanted to name the dogs Waylon and Willie after country music stars Waylon Jennings and Willie Nelson. Wade eventually won the dog naming argument, and so she testified that the micro-chipped dogs were new dogs named after country music stars.

Lizzie seemed most flustered when she testified about her absurd lie that the attack dogs had been euthanized in South Dakota and their remains fed to coyotes. Several times the judge asked her for evidence to corroborate the different aspects of her story, and she and her attorney were constantly interrupting her testimony to frantically search through file folders and stacks of paperwork for the appropriate documentation.

When the City Attorney stood up to cross examine Lizzie, I eagerly leaned forward in my seat. There were blatant discrepancies in her story, and I wanted to see him put her on the hot seat to explain those discrepancies. Unfortunately, as his cross examination continued, I became increasingly apprehensive about how weak and indecisive it seemed, and that he was failing to take advantage of obvious openings to discredit her.

I listened intently as the City attorney asked Lizzie why she had run from the police on the day the dogs were seized. *"It's on now!"* I thought to myself, and I keenly anticipated Lizzie being grilled about resisting arrest.

"I got scared when I looked out my front window and saw several police officers banging on my front gate with their batons!" Lizzie explained. I thought at this point the attorney would confront her with some extremely tough follow up questions, since it seemed to me he had obvious openings you could drive a truck through. I am no legal expert, but I thought that the clear follow up questions were to ask why she ran from the police if she had nothing to hide, and if she realized that resisting arrest and endangering a police officer was a crime. Inexplicably, the city attorney did not ask a single follow up question about the police chase, and moved on to other topics.

"Why the hell isn't he going after her?!" I asked myself in consternation. I could not believe he was not more aggressive in holding Lizzie accountable for her behavior.

The City attorney also failed to explain a key piece of evidence that discredited Lizzie and Wade's story. Prior to the attack, Lizzie had posted a photo of the two mastiffs on her Facebook page with their original names. Months later, after the attack, she posted the exact same photo again on her Facebook page, this time saying they were the "new" dogs with their new country music star names. Meredith had discovered this double posting of the photographs, and it was clearly a key piece of evidence to prove that Lizzie and Wade were lying about the dogs' identities. The City attorney tried to present this in the hearing, but he gave a very muddled and indecisive explanation which the judge was not buying at all.

"Why are you showing this? What is the relevance?" the judge growled at the City Attorney in a deep, gravelly voice, scowling beneath his bushy white eyebrows. The City Attorney stammered nervously, faced with the judge's interrogation and he desperately tried to regroup. He showed no ability to answer the judge's questions in a coherent manner to explain why this evidence was important. The judge seemed like an older man who did not use Facebook, and did not even know what a Facebook page was. Therefore, he did not understand the important meaning of the double posting of the photograph.

In spite of the City attorney's poor performance, I felt confident when I returned to the waiting room after Lizzie concluded her testimony. We all discussed the status of the case and agreed that we were in a strong position for several reasons. Lizzie had been a terrible witness, both with her shady demeanor and the questionable content of her testimony. By contrast, Anne, the dog rescue owner, and Officer Johnson had all been very strong and credible witnesses. Finally, the dogs were micro-chipped to identify them which we felt would make the case a slam dunk.

Anne had a doctor's appointment at the end of the day, so we could not stay to see the end of the hearing and the judge's ruling. I really wanted to see the end because I felt confident about the result, and I was very disappointed that we had to leave. We had scheduled Anne's appointment prior to being informed of the court hearing. We kept the appointment because it was at 5pm, and we assumed the hearing would be finished well before then. We would pay a $100 fine to the doctor if we cancelled with less than 24 hour notice, so we left and waited for Meredith to call us with the verdict.

"I'm afraid I have some bad news!" Meredith said when she called us about an hour after Anne's appointment. "The judge ruled that the City did not provide sufficient evidence that the dogs were the same dogs which had attacked Anne. The burden of proof was on the City, and the City has not proven its case. The judge ruled that the dogs will be released back to Lizzie and Wade as soon as this weekend."

"How the hell did this happen!" I shouted into the phone at Meredith as we were driving home from Anne's appointment. Anne put her hand on my arm to restrain me, and then took the phone from me to talk to Meredith herself. "I agree it's a terrible ruling!" Meredith said to Anne. We were shocked and disgusted with the judge's ruling!

It turned out to be a blessing in disguise that we had to leave before the end of the hearing, because it would have been infuriating to listen to the judge's ruling and then watch Lizzie and Wade celebrate their ugly little triumph. In retrospect, I am afraid I could have been arrested if I had watched the judge's ruling. I probably would have lost my temper at either him or Lizzie and Wade, or both, and then been restrained by courtroom security and charged with contempt of court.

"Somebody will be killed or injured because you were stupid enough to put these dogs back in the hands of criminal dog owners!" I imagined myself shouting at the judge. *"That person's blood will be on your hands!*

Damn right I plead guilty to contempt of court, because I have nothing but contempt for you and your court!"

Sunday October 20th was exactly four months since the dog attack, and we were trying to figure out how to process the horrible injustice of the judge's ruling. We were disgusted at the judge's ruling, and we could not believe that Lizzie and Wade's ridiculous lie could be presented in a court of law and win. I had concocted more credible lies to skip geometry class in high school. The judge who presided over the hearing did a terrible job, and we wondered if there was any way a judge could be fired or impeached for complete incompetence. I sent the following email to friends and family about the verdict.

> *Dark day today. We lost the dog ID case and the owners will be getting the vicious dogs back, maybe as soon as tomorrow or Monday. Technically it was the City of Chicago that lost the case to the owners.*
>
> *This ruling is a disgrace! Our side had three credible witnesses- Anne, a dog rescue owner who originally adopted the dogs to the owners, and officers from animal control. Plus the dogs had been microchipped to ID...*
>
> *Incredibly the judge bought all this bullshit and ruled in their favor. The judge was some grouchy 80 year old fossil who should have retired 20 years ago.*
>
> *We are outraged and disgusted by this ruling. We have complied with every legal requirement asked of us, while the dog owners have complied with nothing and even resisted arrest, yet they end up winning. Clearly there is something fundamentally flawed about the legal system in Chicago and Illinois.*
>
> *Anyway we are going to focus this weekend on positive things like setting up our new house, which is a great space. We need to move on to where this dog attack issue is no longer the major aspect of our lives.*

Monday October 21st was the first business day after the hearing, and I was in an emotional black hole, angry and depressed. I was despondent that we had fought so hard to remove the dogs and to bring Lizzie and Wade to justice and we had lost. As I was driving to work, I planned to stop by the old house first to pick up a few things.

"I can't sugarcoat this one! I'm in a terrible mood!" I said to Anne when I called her as I was driving to the house. "The last place on Earth I want to be is at our old house!" I was terribly worried that the attack dogs would be back lunging and barking at their front fence as they used to, and I dreaded seeing them. The weather reflected my dark, grim mood perfectly, because it was a cold fall morning with low, slate grey skies overhead. A cold steady rain spattered against the windshield of my car, and the windshield wipers beat out a grim rhythm. I drove to the house with my lips tightly pursed and my jaw clenched in a hard line.

"You don't have to stop by the old house today," Anne told me. "You should just go straight into work you're too upset to go over there!"

"I might as well just fucking do it!" I replied bitterly. "We're gonna have to deal with it sooner or later anyway!"

I did stop by the old house that morning and did not see either the dogs or Lizzie and Wade. When I got to work I told Jeanine about the verdict, and she simply replied, "I got nothing." Anne and I both appreciated her response because those three words summed it up. There were no words which could adequately describe or explain the horrible absurdity of the judge's ruling. There were also no better words to describe my state of mind that dark Monday morning.

"I got nothing."

VIGILANTE VISIONS

"Maybe you should throw a package of poisoned meat over the dog owner's fence," one of my co-workers said to me about one week after the hearing. "That would be a way for you to take out those dogs!"

Although I thought he was joking, I began to seriously consider his idea, and to calculate in my mind how I could do it. I figured I could use common rat poison, but how much rat poison would it take to kill two 130 pound bull mastiffs? How would I throw the poisoned meat into their yard undetected? It would have to be around 2-3am because Wade got up very early for his job, around 4am. I visualized myself driving slowly and cautiously down the dark alley behind their house, headlights off, stopping to throw the packages of poisoned ground beef over their fence, then quickly and quietly driving away. Even if I succeeded in accomplishing this undetected, Lizzie and Wade would certainly consider me their number one suspect, so I would have to be prepared for certain retaliation from them.

I have never been one to favor vigilante action, but we had put 100% of our effort into the legal fight, complied with everything the authorities and our attorney had asked us to do, and we ended up with nothing. Our faith in the legal system was deeply shaken, and I began to think that more extreme action was necessary. Besides the poisoned meat, I also considered posting photographs of Anne's bite wounds with warning signs around the neighborhood. We had numerous photographs of Anne's wounds taken by both the ER staff and us, lurid and grotesque images, and I considered blowing these up to poster size and displaying them in our front yard, with warning signs about the dogs pointing to the owner's house. I wanted to display a poster sized photograph of Anne's wounds directly facing Lizzie and Wade's tall balcony, with a sign saying, "*Your dogs did this, her blood is on your hands!*"

In my more reasonable moments, I asked myself if I was becoming mentally unhinged, and I surprised myself with the dark, twisted ideas that began to occupy my mind. They simmered in the darkest corners of my consciousness, so grim that I did not even tell Anne about them. I did discuss with Anne the idea of us taking shooting lessons and buying a gun. I had only fired a gun twice in my life, a 22 rifle at a high school summer camp in Colorado, and a 9mm Gluck pistol at a shooting range in St. Louis, and I had never owned a gun. I had almost no experience with firearms, but since the legal system had so failed to protect us, I began to think that we had to learn to protect ourselves. Our second story back window had a partial view of Lizzie and Wade's yard, and I visualized myself sitting at that window holding a rifle across my knees, patiently waiting for a clear shot at the dogs. I saw Lizzie and Wade rushing out to their yard having heard the gunshot, shocked and dismayed to discover their dead dogs.

"I haven't seen any sign of the dogs," I said to Anne a couple of weeks after the hearing. "I've been to the house almost every day for two weeks and haven't seen them."

"That is strange," Anne replied. "I expected Lizzie and Wade to be parading the dogs all over the neighborhood. This is out of character for them to be so quiet."

Every time we went to the old house we were hyper-alert, listening and watching for any sign of them. Any time we heard a dog bark that sounded large, we wondered if it was them. We had fully expected

Lizzie and Wade to display the dogs in front of us any chance they got to celebrate their ugly little triumph, to rub their legal victory in our faces. We had braced ourselves for the fact that they would put the dogs out every time they saw us, to have them bark at us and intimidate us. So, the silence seemed very strange and we began to wonder what was going on, and why we were not seeing the dogs.

One Monday morning a couple of weeks later a co-worker named Matt approached me on the loading dock and said he had something he wanted to tell me.

"Guess who I met last weekend?!" Matt asked me. "The dog owners! I met them at a bar, where they were circulating a petition about the city releasing the dogs."

Matt had never met Lizzie and Wade before, so he did not know who they were, but he started wondering if the petition was concerning the same dogs that had attacked my wife, and he started asking questions.

"Is your neighbor Drummond Mansfield?" Matt asked Lizzie. When she replied yes, he politely declined to sign the petition.

"I work with Drummond Mansfield. I know what happened with the dog attack," Matt said to Lizzie while handing the petition back to her. "I can't sign this!"

"She was pissed!" Matt said describing Lizzie's reaction, how she angrily walked away from him. Lizzie and Wade glared at Matt the rest of the night, and Wade gave him his usual attempted intimidating stare with crossed arms, a look we had come to know all too well.

"Those people really seem like assholes." Matt concluded. "They seem like they could cause a lot of trouble. I hope they don't become regulars at this bar because I like the place."

What Matt told me got me thinking. Why were Lizzie and Wade circulating a petition if they had already gotten the dogs back? Had Animal Control found an angle, some piece of red tape, to delay releasing the dogs? We knew through Meredith that everyone involved at Animal Control was upset at the judge's ruling, so it made sense that they would use any angle they could to stop the release of the dogs back to the owners. I immediately called Anne and relayed to her what Matt had told me, and Anne called Meredith to notify her of the incident. Meredith immediately started making calls and inquiries.

"The City has appealed the judge's ruling!" Meredith informed Anne the next day. "This is huge! This almost never happens in this type of case!" We were thrilled and relieved to finally receive some legal good news. In addition, Meredith said that Lizzie had a criminal charge pending from when she tried to run over the police officer. We had thought that charge may have been dropped, but it was not. Lizzie and Wade were also still on the hook for all legal expenses for both the dog case and the criminal charges related to the police chase, so they were racking up some serious legal bills. They were finally beginning to see some consequences to their dreadful behavior.

It had been an amazing stroke of good luck that Matt had encountered Lizzie and Wade circulating the petition, because otherwise we may never have known what was happening. We were very thankful to him for notifying us. We began to hope against hope that the legal battle was finally starting to shift our way.

In early November, one of Anne's co-workers told her that she had been watching Live News and had seen a story on the evening news about the dog attack case. Apparently, Lizzie and Wade had taken their case to the media. I called Meredith to notify her of this new development, and she already knew about it.

"Live News called our office and we said no comment, because of the ongoing legal proceedings," Meredith explained to me. "I watched the story and I thought it was just a silly, puff piece. It has no legal consequence that we need to worry about."

Jeanine emailed us a link to the story with the subject line *"Really?! She is Insane!"* I watched the news clip when I got home from work, and it was a very incomplete and inaccurate story which was completely slanted to Lizzie and Wade's perspective. Both Lizzie and her attorney were interviewed for the story, and they both said that they had won the dog ID hearing and should get the dogs back.

"Just give the dogs back," they were both quoted as saying. The TV footage showed Lizzie being interviewed in front of her house, her round face and shiny black hair illuminated by fall sunlight. In the background was the black, metal fence and front yard where we used

to see the dogs leaping and lunging, and where the dog attack had taken place.

The story completely downplayed the severity of the attack, describing it simply as a dog bite with no mention of the fact that Anne was almost killed and scarred for life. They posted a brief written statement from animal control saying that they had evidence to believe the dogs were the same dogs involved in the attack, but otherwise it was a complete puff piece in favor of Lizzie and Wade.

"I voluntarily removed the dogs to make the dog attack victim more comfortable," Lizzie was quoted as saying. This was the worst part of the story because it was a shameless lie which could not be farther from the truth. They had done everything possible to avoid removing the dogs, to the point of resisting arrest and lying under oath in court. Lizzie and Wade had subjected us to constant intimidation and harassment, to the point where we carried pepper spray every time we made a trip to the old house. We had felt extremely threatened by them ever since I had my big argument with them. The tension and stress were excruciating for the entire two months we continued to live next door to them, before we made the extremely difficult decision that we had to move from our home of 14 years. Watching Lizzie smugly lie on television was infuriating!

I was outraged when I finished watching the Live News story! Besides the dog attack itself, I had never been so angry about anything. My fury was compounded by the fact that Meredith wanted us to keep quiet about the case, because anything we said could compromise us legally. I really wanted to call Live News and give them a piece of my mind, but Meredith strongly advised me not to.

"How can Lizzie's attorney go on TV grandstanding for an interview, while Meredith just says no comment and tells us to keep quiet?!" I asked Anne angrily. "I'm getting really worried that Meredith isn't tough enough! We need a fucking attorney who will fight for us!"

"She's just seeing it as a lawyer," Anne tried to reason with me. "As long as the story doesn't legally affect our case she doesn't care."

"I think Meredith should care, legally or not!" I shouted back. "I'd like to see her start to get pissed off about all this!"

I was in a rage the night after I watched the Live News story. My anger was so intense that Anne and our dogs were afraid of me, even though nothing was directed toward them. I cannot remember exactly what I said or did, although I vaguely recall kicking over a chair or a lamp. I do remember that I did not sleep a wink all night, that I spent the night furiously pacing our house. Our dogs slouched in a corner of our living room with their tails between their legs and moved away from me any time I came in their direction. Anne considered taking the dogs and going to a friend's house for the night.

Although Anne was unhappy with the Live News story, she was much less angry about it than I was, and she seemed to share Meredith's view that it was ultimately meaningless bullshit. Anne seemed to understand Meredith better than I did, and, as tensions developed between Meredith and me, Anne did most of the communication with her. Part of my disconnect I had with Meredith was her personality, because she was a very cool, reserved young woman who did not show much emotion, and I perceived this as her not being invested in our case.

This was in fact not true. Increasingly, Meredith had begun to take our case personally, because Lizzie was attacking her on Facebook. Lizzie had posted comments on Facebook criticizing Meredith', saying she was an ambulance chaser who used a dog rescue organization she volunteered for to funnel dog attack cases to her law firm. Of course this was untrue, but it was typical of Lizzie's behavior - to use any tactic, no matter how sleazy, vicious, or dishonest, to attack us and anyone associated with us. I believe this made Meredith take the case more personally and increased her resolve, but she never showed it through her cool demeanor.

With great difficulty, I complied with Meredith's advice not to talk about the case, and I never called Live News, although the order to remain silent was driving me crazy. I had not made any public statements but I had sent voluminous emails to family and friends. I had a long chain of emails which I had sent to family and friends as the events unfolded, which I started shortly after the attack when I notified everyone about it and Anne being in the hospital. Since then,

I had continued to send regular updates as the situation developed. These were mostly directed to people from my side of the aisle. In the immediate aftermath of the attack, I had called Anne's mother and sister from the hospital, but once she began to recover, she called her family and friends herself.

One of these emails was about the Live News story where I sent a link to family and friends. One friend responded with genuine anger after watching the clip, and it was gratifying to know that someone shared my anger, that I was not crazy for being so outraged. Sally emailed me, "*I watched the video. I am outraged on your behalf, Drummond!!! I also just love how it says the neighbor was BITTEN!!! As if it was one little bite. That attack sure was downplayed. OUTRAGEOUS AND UNBELIEVABLE!!! This makes me SO MAD!!*"

Meredith was not happy with me about this email chain, because even though they were personal emails to family and friends, they were potentially admissible in court.

"I wasn't crazy about your email about the hearing," She told me, referring to the email where I wrote that "*the judge was a grouchy old fossil who should have retired 20 years ago.*" On a practical level, it created more work for her, because she had to read through all the emails and decide which parts were admissible and had to be disclosed to the opposing attorneys. Tensions had increased in our relationship, because I was unhappy about the gag order Meredith had placed on us, and she was unhappy about the extensive emails I had sent.

It felt intrusive and violating to have my personal email correspondence sent to the dog owner's sleazy attorney, for him to find anything I said that could be used against us. I also felt like it was unfair that these emails could be used against us, because the only reason I wrote them was to reach out to family and friends for support during crisis. It felt dirty that emails which were sent with innocent intentions could potentially be used against us in a court of law. Jeanine said it best, "It's like someone stole your diary!"

"Drummond doesn't want to jeopardize our case. He's just extremely upset!" Anne said to Meredith. "He should be!" Meredith replied. I really appreciated that Anne had defended me about the email chain, because I would have felt terrible if I had written anything that would hurt our case. I really needed her to back me up and she did.

I began writing this novel during this phase when the legal gag order was in place, and because of the gag order, I could not use a computer. The early drafts of this novel were written with good old-fashioned pen and paper. I filled up a couple of legal pads which I kept carefully tucked away in a desk drawer when I was not writing. It seemed strangely appropriate to the whole situation that to begin writing this story, I had to go underground and off the grid.

Our faith in both the criminal justice system and the news media was seriously compromised in the aftermath of the disgraceful dog ID ruling and the biased media story. Back to back during the same month we had been betrayed by both the justice system and the news media, and our confidence in both was deeply shaken. I understood this before on an intellectual level. I have long been skeptical of the media for inaccuracy and bias. But after the Live News story I became a skeptic on a much more visceral level. I developed a cynical attitude toward every story I read or watched, and always wondered what part of the story had been overlooked, distorted, or were outright lies.

The City ultimately made a deal with Lizzie and Wade where the dogs were removed to a shelter in Wisconsin, with the stipulation that if they were ever seen again in the City of Chicago, they would be impounded and euthanized immediately. They were given new microchips to avoid any farther confusion about their identity. The Wisconsin dog shelter specialized in dogs with major behavior problems, such as dogs which had been rescued from dog fighting rings. Ironically, those were the exact terms of the original banishment order from the City. If Lizzie and Wade had simply cooperated with the original order, none of the subsequent drama would have happened. The search warrant, the police chase, the dog ID hearings, none of that needed to happen. It all could have been avoided if they had simply cooperated with the investigation to begin with.

EYES ON THE PRIZE

I know this is hard but eye on the prize! As in "don't get mad, get even" as a strategy. You will get a chance at some point in time to counter their crazy lies. Til then, eye on the prize!!!

This email was sent by an old family friend named Melissa, replying to my email about losing the dog ID hearing. She was attempting to remind us that our lawsuit was the most important aspect of our legal battle, ultimately more important than the dog ID hearings. This reply from Melissa was very helpful in directing us to focus on our most important legal issue, and to move forward from the setback of the dog ID hearing.

The dog attack gave us a crash course in the legal system. I was 50 years old at the time of the attack, and we had never hired an attorney except for when we bought the Humboldt Park house. One thing we learned was that the legal system liked to keep everything separate. At one point, there were three different legal actions in progress, all separate from each other. There was the lawsuit between us and Lizzie and Wade's homeowner's insurance company, the dog identification case which was Chicago Animal Control versus Lizzie and Wade, and the criminal case against Lizzie for resisting arrest during the seizure of the dogs. The criminal case we had nothing to do with, since we were not home at the time and did not witness anything. We never did find out what happened with the criminal charges. We were hoping that Lizzie would do some jail time, at least long enough for us to finish our move, but apparently she did not because she always seemed to be home.

Right after the New Year's holiday in January, Meredith emailed us saying that both our depositions would be scheduled within that month. Since Anne was the attack victim hers was the primary deposition, and mine was more supportive. Meredith eventually decided that my deposition was not necessary, and that they only needed Anne's testimony.

"I'm upset that Meredith doesn't want my deposition," I said to Anne. "I want to tell my side of the story. Sometimes I feel like I don't even matter in this situation." Anne and I had taken turns playing the role of supportive spouse, first when Anne's father passed away and later when my mother passed away. We both had found that role to be very difficult, and that the spouse sometimes felt lost with all the attention being paid to the grieving partner. I had begun to feel that way with the dog attack, that all the attention was on Anne as the victim, and that what I had gone through was of no consequence. I was also chafing under Meredith's legal gag order.

"I think you're lucky that you don't have to be deposed," Anne replied. "This is a lot of pressure! I'm really worried about it!"

This was true that Anne felt tremendous anxiety and pressure in the days leading up to her deposition. She worried that she would make some mistake in her testimony which would jeopardize any potential financial settlement. Her deposition was scheduled on a cold, clear January afternoon. I left work early to pick her up and drive her to Meredith's office, in a tall high rise building in downtown Chicago. Anne practically had a panic attack as we were driving downtown, with her hands shaking uncontrollably.

"You're going to do great!" I said to Anne attempting to reassure her. “You did really well in your testimony at the dog ID hearing, and you’ll do even better here!” Legally I was not allowed to attend the deposition, so I dropped her off at Meredith’s office and went to do some work at the old house until she was finished.

The attorneys for Lizzie and Wade’s insurance company were respectful and non-confrontational in their questioning. Anne really cut loose and told the whole story. She talked about all the harassment, abuse, and other problems we had associated with Lizzie and Wade and the dog attack. She held nothing back, and she came off as a credible witness.

“Do you need to take photographs of Anne’s scars?” Meredith asked the insurance company attorneys.

“That’s ok, you can just send us photos later,” the insurance attorneys replied. “If Anne’s not comfortable she doesn’t have to show us her scars.”

“That’s not a problem,” Anne said, pulling up her skirt to reveal the scars on her thighs. “You can take photographs right now.” The insurance attorneys seemed shocked but kept their reaction muted and reserved, and they quickly whipped out their phones to photograph her scars.

Anne glanced across the room to Meredith, who gave her a brief subtle nod, and a faint hint of a smile played across her lips. By this stage in the case, Anne and Meredith understood each other very well, and Anne knew what that nod meant. Anne knew that Meredith was screaming in her head “Yes! Yes! Let them see your scars!” Meredith wanted the insurance attorneys to see the actual scars, not just photographs, because she thought it would be a powerful statement influencing them to offer a good settlement.

Lizzie had lied to her own insurance company, saying that only one dog was involved in the attack, when it was legally documented from the dog ID hearing that there were three dogs. The two huge bull mastiffs had done most of the damage, but the smaller yellow Labrador mix had also attacked. We were amazed that she would try to lie about something that was legally documented, but we had learned to not be surprised by any of her behavior. Lizzie had a mysterious knack for getting people to believe her lies, which seemed transparent to us, lies that any intelligent and reasonable person would question, even if they had no background knowledge of what happened. She had succeeded in fooling a judge, Live News, a dog rescue shelter, and the Buddy Project charity organization, so it made sense that she would lie to her own insurance company as well. Anne and I were baffled about how Lizzie could be so successful at tricking and manipulating people. Even when we were friendly with her, we did not see her as an exceptionally charismatic person, who could captivate people with her charm. She was not strikingly beautiful, so she could not blind people with her good looks. Her lies themselves strained credulity. What was her secret?

"How does Lizzie get away with so much?!" I asked Anne in frustration. "It makes no sense whatsoever!"

"If she wasn't so gross and disgusting, I would think she was running around City Hall giving blowjobs!" I joked.

"There are probably some guys who would like it," Anne replied.

"I bet you're right," I said. "But I guarantee you I wouldn't let her nasty mouth anywhere near my business!"

On February 12th, Meredith called Anne and told her that the insurance company had made an offer and that the case had been settled.

"Why did Meredith agree to the settlement without consulting us first?" I asked Anne. We were upset that Meredith had accepted the offer without asking us, and Anne called her and asked her the same question. The answer was that the insurance company had offered the entire value of the homeowner's insurance policy and because they had offered us the maximum value, the settlement was automatic. There was no option of the lawsuit going to trial.

We initially were disappointed, because we felt that we needed more compensation than the insurance policy, given the trauma of the whole experience. We were hoping that the settlement would cover the cost of plastic surgery for the scarring. Anne had gone to a plastic surgeon who gave her an estimate for the scars on her thighs. This would happen approximately two years later, because the scars needed to heal that long before surgery could be done. The plastic surgeon meticulously measured and documented every one of Anne's scars, and counted over 90 scars in total.

Upon reflection, we realized that this settlement offer was the best we could have gotten given the money available. Insurance companies have a reputation for finding ways not to pay out claims. So, we felt it was indicative of the strength of our case that their insurance company offered the maximum value so quickly and easily. We imagined that after Anne's deposition, their attorneys had gone back to the insurance company and said something like, "Houston we have a problem! We need to just settle and wash our hands of this one!"

Lizzie and Wade were blue collar people who did not have an affluent homeowner's insurance policy, so the settlement was the best we could hope for. Plus, if we had gone after any of their personal assets, we would have had to go through collections agencies trying to get them to pay. Given their pattern of behavior, and their hatred of us, getting them to pay a dime would have been like wringing blood out of a stone. The settlement offer was not what we would have hoped for in a perfect world, but it was the best possible resolution given the legal and financial realities.

Early in the morning the day after the settlement was announced, Anne received a call from Lizzie. Anne did not answer, since we had long since discontinued any communication with her and Wade. Lizzie did not leave a message, but we were sure she was calling because she had just been informed of the settlement and was angry about it. Meredith had told us that the settlement wiped out Lizzie and Wade's homeowners' insurance policy. Most likely their insurance company would drop them, and in the future, homeowners' insurance would be much more expensive, if they were able to get insurance at all.

Within a week after the settlement was announced, the insurance company cut our attorneys' a check. Our attorneys' fee was 1/3 of the total settlement amount, so we received a check for 2/3 of the total, minus some the hospital expenses. It was by far the single largest dollar amount we had ever received in a check. It was a significant amount of money which we would put toward Anne's plastic surgery if she chose to go that route or invest some other way if not. However, it was also not so much money that Anne and I could quit our jobs and live on a yacht the rest of our lives.

"The only bad thing about settling so quickly and easily is that you never got to depose Lizzie," we said to Meredith when we picked up the check at her office.

"Damn!" Meredith replied, snapping her fingers. Both Lizzie and Wade were scheduled for depositions by Meredith, but their insurance company offered the settlement before either one took place. Anne, Meredith, and I all regretted this, because we were all looking forward to Meredith deposing them. Although we wanted her to depose Wade, we were licking our collective chops at the prospect of Meredith deposing Lizzie. Given Meredith's cool, calculating demeanor, her deposition would have been a surgical dissection of Lizzie's web of lies. Meredith was angry at the personal attacks from Lizzie she had suffered on Facebook, so she was chomping at this bit for her deposition. All three of us had been looking forward to Meredith putting Lizzie on the hot seat, and we were all disappointed that it never happened.

"You all did a great job for us!" Anne and I said to Meredith and our colleagues as we said goodbye to them. "Thank you so much!" It seemed strange that after all the crazy twists and turns, suddenly, in the blink of an eye, the legal part of our journey was all over. Although there had been some tensions with Meredith along the road, in the end, we felt like she and her law firm guided us through the legal labyrinth in the best way possible.

"This traffic is a bitch!" I said as we drove through downtown after leaving Meredith's office. "I don't know if we're going to make it to the bank before it closes." Because it was such a large amount, we wanted to go straight to the bank and deposit it immediately in a new account. Anne and I were not well organized about personal paperwork, and we did not want this check to get misplaced, lost or stolen. Meredith's office was in downtown Chicago, and our financial advisor's office was in a bank branch on the northwest side of the city. It was the height of downtown afternoon rush hour, and traffic was crawling at an excruciatingly slow pace.

Prior to picking up the check, we had met with a financial advisor. We explained that the money was earmarked for Anne's plastic surgery on her scars, if she chose that option, and that this would not happen for a couple of years because of the healing time required. Because of that, we decided on a very low risk option of placing the money in a 2 year, CD account. There were stock market funds that could have earned us a lot more money, but were also much higher risk, and we could not afford to lose any of the money until Anne decided on her plastic surgery option.

"I guess money really does talk," I said to Anne after we finally made it to the bank. "I've never seen a bank staff be that attentive!" We were amused that they had been so attentive because we had arrived after the closing time and they had stayed open late to accommodate us. The receptionist knew who we were before we had even introduced ourselves, and we were ushered into the financial advisor's office immediately, even though it was after closing time. But we also understood that we did not really have the money. Anne's plastic surgery could easily consume the entire settlement amount or more.

We did some research on a website called *"Dogsbite.org"*, which posted testimonials from dog bite victims all over the country. We learned that there were many serious dog mauling incidents, and that there were many dangerous animals owned by irresponsible people. A teenage boy in Tennessee had both his ears ripped off by a pit bull. An attack in Texas was eerily similar to Anne's. The attack occurred at an RV trailer park campground, where a woman went over to a neighbor's trailer to do her a favor, and was mauled by a pit bull that the neighbor owned. Because the woman did not own the property where the attack occurred, the victim had no legal recourse, and could not even find an attorney to take her case. Unlike Anne, this woman in Texas was unable to protect her face. She had serious bite wounds and scars on her face. When she was out in public with her husband he often got dirty looks from people who assumed that he was abusing her because of the scars.

Dogsbite.org focused on attacks by pit bulls, but the dogs which attacked Anne were officially identified as bull mastiffs. Pit bulls are not the only dangerous dog breed.

A woman named Caress Garten (pronounced Karis) was mauled by two pit bulls in a state park in Indiana. She lost part of her left leg, and afterward she wrote a memoir called *"On Behalf of Innocents."* The owner of the two dogs who attacked her was involved in dog fighting. He had given the dogs multiple names to create confusion with the authorities. Ms. Garten wrote that this was a common tactic among dog fighters to fight their dogs under different names, and we thought that was strikingly similar to the lies Lizzie and Wade had told about the dogs names in the dog ID hearing. The legal penalty for the dog owner in this case was a $12.50 leash law violation. Ms. Garten was able to use her story to influence the Indiana state legislature to pass a bill toughening dog attack laws, something I hope to do in Chicago with this novel.

Anthony Solesky was the father of a boy who was mauled by a pit bull while playing baseball and he wrote a memoir entitled *"Dangerous by Default."* After the attack the dog owner attempted to intimidate the boy, threatening him not to tell his parents, and he never called the police or ambulance. We found it striking that in both their memoirs and my novel the dog owners behaved disgracefully after the attack.

We had two realizations. We were extremely fortunate to get the settlement we did, given that other dog mauling victims had often gotten nothing, and dangerous dog laws needed serious reform. It was ridiculous that the attack was treated legally as a mere liability on Lizzie and Wade's property, as if she had fallen through a faulty porch railing.

Lizzie had written the following in her note which she taped to our mailbox, when she accused Anne of trespassing.

My friends that arrived at the scene of the accident, which is exactly what it was, an accident, asked me at the time, if I wanted to press charges and I declined in the spirit of being neighborly.

I have recently changed my mind regarding that topic as I am tired of being treated as a criminal, and as if I had done something wrong; I did nothing wrong.

Lizzie could not be more misguided with what she wrote. The dog attack was no accident. It was a CRIME! We treated Lizzie as a criminal because SHE IS A CRIMINAL! It is a miscarriage of justice that the law does not view her as a criminal despite her almost killing a woman. Rather than having done nothing wrong, she did everything wrong, and she should have faced felony charges as a consequence! Dangerous dog owners should be prosecuted as criminals!

Lizzie and Wade should have been charged with assault with a deadly weapon just as if they had attacked Anne themselves with a gun or knife. If Anne had been killed they should have been charged with criminally negligent homicide. Chicago Animal Control should have removed and impounded the dogs immediately after the attack. Lizzie and Wade should never have been allowed to keep the animals on their property at their own discretion, after such a serious attack. They never should have been given the window of opportunity to make their bullshit claim that they were different dogs.

Through the *DogsBite.org* website, we learned that there were many attacks by dangerous dogs all across the country, and that often the owners were highly irresponsible and/or dangerous people. There is precious little media attention paid to this nationwide problem. In terms of holding dog owners accountable, and achieving justice for the victims of dog attacks, the laws regarding dangerous dogs are woefully inadequate!

THE TAX FIGHT

"You're such a dick!" Anne exclaimed to me repeatedly on the phone. "I can't believe you're making me do taxes by myself!"

"It's your own damned fault!" I shot back every time. "You should have listened to my idea about filing for an extension!"

The April 15th tax deadline was looming the next week. Like most Americans, Anne and I hated doing our taxes, which seemed to get more complicated with each passing year. Every year we promised ourselves we would start on them early, but we dreaded the process and invariably, would procrastinate until the last day. This was the worst year yet, because we were still in the thick of the move from hell. We were exhausted, stressed out and overwhelmed, and the thought of doing our taxes sounded miserable.

I thought I had read somewhere that there was an option to file for an extension, and I asked the accountant at my work about it.

"It's easy," the accountant explained when I asked him about it. "All you have to do is fill out a form and make sure you submit it by April 15th." He emailed me the forms which I forwarded to our personal email, then went home at the end of the day to discuss it with Anne. I felt pleased because I thought I had found a solution which would take some pressure off us during a terribly difficult time in our lives.

"Absolutely not!" was Anne's response when I floated her the idea. "We have to get taxes done! We are NOT filing for an extension!"

"Why the hell not?!" I exclaimed to Anne. I felt blindsided and angry at her response because I had assumed she would like the idea or at least be willing to consider it.

"I talked to a CERTIFIED PUBLIC ACCOUNTANT about it!" I continued, strongly emphasizing those three words. "He said all we have to do is fill out a form by April 15th and that there is no financial penalty."

Anne continued to strongly resist the idea and I quickly became extremely frustrated with her. I was upset because she did not offer any coherent explanation as to why she was so resistant to the idea of an extension.

"You cannot do one goddamned thing to make our lives easier!" I shouted at her. "You're genetically incapable of it! You always have to do everything the hardest way possible!"

On the last Sunday morning before the April 15th deadline Anne said she wanted to work on taxes.

"I want to work on taxes this morning," she said. "We need to get this done!"

"I'm not doing taxes this morning!" I told her. "I want to file for an extension and I have other stuff I want to do! I'll fill out the extension form if you want me to but that's the only work I'm doing on taxes."

Anne worked on taxes alone that Sunday, and continued working on them alone the following Monday, when she had time off for spring break while I went to work. She was furious about spending her spring break time doing taxes alone, and I was equally angry that she had shot down my idea about filing for an extension, while offering no explanation as to why. I had no idea what she was thinking, or why she would be so adamant about not filing for an extension.

We had been arguing a lot during this phase of the move, but this was the worst one. It was one of the worst arguments we ever had in our 24 years together. It was a maddening circular argument where

Anne complained over and over that I was making her do taxes by herself, and I countered over and over that she should have listened to my idea about the extension.

"Maybe we should just get a divorce!" Anne said to me on the phone. "It might be easier than this!" The word divorce had started to creep into our arguments and I began to call it the d-word.

"It's devastating and heartbreaking to think that we've come so far and survived so much, but in the end we might not make it," I replied to her in a text message from work. I felt as if I had fallen into a deep well of sadness. I had no idea why Anne was being so obstinate and stubborn about the tax extension, and I really had no idea of how to deal with her. I decided to call one of Anne's teaching friends named Christine for some advice.

"I have never done this before!" I said to Christine. "In 24 years I have never called a friend in the middle of an argument. I just don't know where Anne is right now, I have no idea how to deal with her! I could have called one of my own friends, but they don't know Anne like you do. I needed to talk to someone who understands Anne."

Anne and I had a strong commitment to privacy as a couple. We were always very careful to keep our family and friends out of any arguments and issues we had. It was a very big deal that I called Christine, because under normal circumstances I never would have done so. But we were not living in normal circumstances, and I was desperate and totally lost about what to do. The Anne who I was arguing with was a total stranger.

"I think maybe you guys just need a break from each other," Christine advised me. "If one of you wants to come to my house for a couple of days, you're welcome. That might help cool things down and then you can work it out." Christine took the call in stride and was very calm and supportive.

"I'm not asking you to take sides," I told her. "You can even side with Anne if you want, I don't care. I just needed to talk to someone who understands Anne, because right now I just don't know how to handle her. Thank you so much for talking to me!"

"Do not call my friends!" Anne angrily texted me when I told her

I called Christine. I texted her back saying that my conversation with Christine was positive, but Anne was not buying it. She felt that my phone call to her friend was a major violation of a privacy pact between us. She later apologized to Christine that I had called her.

"You do realize this is my Spring Break!" Anne wrote me in another angry text when I went to work on Monday. *"I have been under so much pressure! I needed this vacation so bad, and instead I'm spending it fighting with you and working on taxes alone! You're an asshole!"*

This text hit home to me because I knew how much Anne had been through and I very much wanted her to relax and take care of herself. It made me feel bad that I was robbing her of this opportunity, and I backed off on my hard line about not helping her with the taxes.

"Ok, I'll see if I can get off work early and come home to help you finish," I relented as our fight cooled down and my anger dissipated.

In the end, we got our taxes in on time. I came home and helped Anne tie up the loose ends, and then rushed to the post office and got taxes mailed before the post office closed at 6pm.

After the smoke had cleared from our argument, we were composed enough to discuss it in a reasonable manner, and we both came to some important realizations about how we felt, and how our tax argument was really about deeper issues.

"Last year was such a horrible year!" Anne explained to me. "I just have to put it behind me and finishing taxes was part of that!"

Her explanation made perfect sense to me, and I finally understood why she had been so obstinate and unwilling to compromise about the tax extension. Finishing last year's taxes was emotional for her because it was a step in putting a terrible traumatic year behind her and moving forward.

"I could have compromised about the extension," I replied to Anne explaining my side of the argument. "But I was really mad at you that you didn't listen to me. That's why I was being such a jerk about not helping you. After the attack, you promised you were going to listen to me more, but you wouldn't even discuss the extension."

We both realized that the fight was about deeper problems related to the dog attack, and that our taxes were only the surface concern, a spark which ignited the tinder box of the deeper issues.

Ask me now if I think it was a good idea to call Christine, and I would say no. It was a mistake, and I now feel embarrassed about it. However, I do not beat myself up too much for this mistake. At the time I was under tremendous strain, and I did not know what to do.

In retrospect, I should have called Jeanine since she was my trusted confidante during the whole situation. But Jeanine had only met Anne once while Christine and Anne had worked together extensively, so because of that I thought Christine could offer more insight. I called Christine because I was lost and desperate, in a terrible situation. It was a moment of weakness because I was starting to crack under the pressure.

Our discussion prior to the dog attack about the dogs being dangerous had become the most painful and conflicted issue in our relationship. I was angry and resentful that Anne had not listened to me, that she had almost gotten herself killed and put us in a terrible situation.

At the same time, I felt extremely guilty for having these feelings of resentment. This poor woman, my wife, my life partner, my best friend, had been scarred for life and had long term physical and emotional pain. How could I resent her when she had been through so much? What kind of person was I to give her that additional burden? She had been punished enough for several lifetimes, and she certainly did not need me to tell her I told you so.

"I really need you to forgive me for not listening to you about the dogs," Anne said to me several times. "I was just trying to help somebody out. I never wanted all this to happen."

"I have forgiven you," I reassured Anne. "I know you had only good intentions."

"I don't think so," she replied skeptically. "It doesn't feel like it."

Anne felt a tremendous amount of guilt and regret that she had opened the door to watch the dogs, and she was right. I had not fully forgiven her. Several times, I thought I had forgiven her, but then my resentment would resurface in stressful moments or arguments. My resentment was like a dark seed that lay dormant within me but would strike out in unexpected moments which surprised even me. Anne understood all too well that she had made the biggest mistake of her life when she opened that door to watch the dogs. She had a deep sense of regret which was a heavy burden upon her soul.

Often, my resentment came out when I was moving Anne's stuff, exacerbated by the fact that I was moving it under the lurking, threatening, obsessively watchful eye of Lizzie. During the tax fight, Anne had said the word divorce.

"If you were going to divorce me, you should have done it before the move!" I snapped back at her bitterly. "You should have done it before I had to move all your shit!"

Lizzie of course was creepily watching our every move. She seized on the weakness of ours that we had too much stuff and she started calling us hoarders. I had obtained several "*We Call Police*" signs from the alderman's office, and I taped five of them directly facing Lizzie and Wade's house.

"*I am tired of being treated as a criminal, and as if I had done something wrong*," Lizzie had written in the note we thought she had taped to our mailbox, so I knew that the "*We Call Police*" signs facing her house would get under her skin. Sure enough, it did, and she responded with a note taped to her window saying "*We call police on sicko hoarders.*" It was written in blue marker, with crude, blocky letters, as though it had been written by an angry child. Anne and I laughed at the note.

Although she did not talk much about it, I knew that there was a part of Anne that wanted to simply run away from her whole life and start over. There was a part of her that wanted to get in the car and start driving, to just keep on driving and never look back. I knew this included driving away from me. This knowledge broke my heart, but I began to wonder if this was the best thing for her. Maybe it would be best if Anne just drove away to a place far removed from our terrible situation.

I had done the best I could in supporting Anne after the attack, but I also served as a reminder of the attack and everything she had been through. Perhaps my best was simply not good enough to heal the wounds that scarred her heart and soul. Maybe it would be best for Anne if she was completely removed from me. It might help her with healing and moving on, where she could be free of the terrible burden of guilt and regret she carried within her. If she drove that car as far as she could, perhaps she could someday drive out from under the dark cloud of sorrow that loomed over her.

During our 24 years together three of our four parents had passed away. We had learned that we were unable to have children, and went through five failed rounds of IVF and three miscarriages. We had put down four beloved family pets. But maybe in this situation we had finally encountered something we as a couple could not overcome.

We kept a card on our dresser which was my favorite card Anne ever got me. It depicted the shadow of a man and woman holding hands, cast across a dirt pathway. The man's shadow cut across the picture long and straight and the woman's shadow flared out in the shape of a skirt. The caption simply said *"Journey"*.

I looked at this card every morning, and I wondered if after 24 years together as a couple our journey together had finally come to an end.

Our journey together had begun in January 1990 when we first met. We were both art students at Bowling Green State University near Toledo Ohio, and we met in a printmaking class which we were both taking. We hit it off beautifully and began talking to each other at length and hanging out as friends. Our sense of humor crackled like electricity between us. Anne liked to read jokes from Laffy Taffy wrappers to the class, silly, stupid jokes, but I found it endearing.

We did not actually become a couple until April 1990, and I almost blew my chances with Anne by being too cautious. The reason for my caution was that prior to Anne I had terrible relationships with women. I had three consecutive relationships prior to Anne which were twisted love-hate relationships which had ended bitterly, and I was angry and cynical about the way my girlfriends had treated me. I was conflicted with a lot of guilt and remorse, because I had been no angel myself.

I felt guilty toward my first girlfriend who was the most serious and long term of my pre-Anne relationships. We were together for five years in our early twenties. Our breakup was very sad and painful for both of us, and I had many regrets about how I had handled it.

These breakups were followed by a period of almost two years where I had no woman in my life at all. I lived alone, in a series of shitty basement apartments, with way too much time on my hands to brood over my relationship failures. One day, I saw a funny bumper sticker which was a mock classified dating advertisement. It read, *"Moody temperamental bitch looking for kind considerate guy to have love-hate relationship with."* When I read it as the woman drove past, I felt like I should run after her car shouting, "Stop, let me in! We're made for each other!" The entire history of my pre-Anne relationships with women had been summed up in that bumper sticker.

On a chilly evening in March 1990, Anne sat on the couch with a blanket over her legs, while I sat in an armchair on the other side of the room. "Are you cold?" Anne asked me. "Do you want some blanket?"

"No thanks, I'm not cold," I replied. I left soon afterward to go back to my own apartment. About an hour later a light bulb went off in my head that Anne had been hinting that she was offering me the blanket because she wanted me to sit next to her. I spent the rest of the evening berating myself in the mirror for being such an idiot who had blown any chance I had with her.

"What the hell is wrong with you!?" I chastised myself over and over. Simultaneously, Anne called one of her girlfriends crying, "I don't think Drummond's interested in me. I don't know what else I can do!" When we are 100 years old in our rocking chairs in a nursing home, Anne will still not let me live that one down.

I finally worked up the courage to touch Anne while we were sitting in her apartment during April 1990. I reached out to touch her hand tentatively and nervously, and she squeezed my hand in return. Eric Clapton's song *"Wonderful Tonight"* played on the radio in the background. All night long, we slowly and sensually explored each other on the carpeted floor of her living room. Her apartment had a sliding glass door in front, dimly illuminated by a street lamp at the dark end of the street which cast a soft glow into the room. The first time we touched each other, it felt brand new and somehow as though we had known each other forever, and we had no inhibitions. My previous relationships had been characterized by a lot of adolescent awkwardness, but there was none of that with Anne. Both physically and emotionally, we were two streams who flowed together in-to each other like clear, fresh water. Our relationship was so smooth and effortless, and I had never experienced that sensation of connecting so naturally and easily with another person.

Bowling Green, Ohio was a small college town located in pancake flat farmland about an hour from Toledo. On quiet nights it could be desolate, without a person, a car or even a dog barking to break the silence. When I met Anne, I lived in a musty basement apartment underneath a crumbling white mansion with a large curved veranda. Late one night in May 1990, we were returning to my apartment from a college bar after having just seen a great musical comedy act called the Village Idiots. Absolutely nobody was out, and Anne and I walked down the middle of the four-lane main street with no concern about cars or other pedestrians. As we neared my apartment, Anne grabbed my hand and started skipping, and I joined in to catch up. We skipped the remaining two blocks to my apartment down the middle of main street. Our only company was vacant street lights and a round, orange neon sign from a closed Sunoco gas station. The street was silent except for the scuffing of our feet on the pavement as we skipped, and the sound of our happy laughter.

Although everything was going beautifully with Anne, I did not trust it. The cynicism I built up from my past relationship failures continued to haunt me. No matter how good it was with Anne, I was waiting for the other shoe to drop, and I hesitated in committing to our relationship. A couple of my earlier relationships had started off well, but quickly collapsed like a house of cards. This made me worry that the same thing might happen with Anne - that she might prove to be just another mirage in the desert of my relationships. In September 1990, I took a month- long trip alone to California, staying with friends near the San Francisco region. During this trip, I discovered that I missed Anne desperately and I could not wait to come home to her. I spent much of my trip writing long letters to her.

Returning home, I drove as many hours as I could stay awake, because I was excited and eager to get back and see Anne. Late one evening, I was approaching Albuquerque, New Mexico, when my car engine suddenly went silent and stopped running. I drifted off to a stop on the side of the Interstate highway. A few miles away the lights of Albuquerque glowed against the night sky, and a baleful yellow moon hung low over the desert. I tried to sleep in my car overnight, but 18 wheelers were constantly roaring past, engine braking on the slope into Albuquerque, kicking up wind which shook my car and woke me up. The following morning, I hitchhiked into Albuquerque to find a tow truck and a mechanic. I ended up stranded in Albuquerque for four days, because the auto mechanics had to lift the entire engine out of the car to replace a broken timing chain which had caused the breakdown.

"I miss you so much!" I said to Anne calling her from a battered pay phone in a dark corner of the motel parking lot where I was staying, which was dimly lit by a flickering neon sign that read "Sky Vue Motel." The motel I stayed at was seedy and run down, looking like a setting for a David Lynch movie, and every night I called Anne collect. Of course, this was before the era of texting and instant communication, so our one collect pay phone call each evening was our only contact, and we both lingered on the phone as long as we could trying to stay connected. "I miss you too!" Anne replied. "I'm so worried about you being stranded out there! I can't wait for you to get home!"

I was flat broke, and my parents had to wire me $500+ cash for the car repairs, which I was embarrassed about because I was really trying to establish financial independence at the time. Finally, after four days, the mechanics got my car fixed, and I drove home apprehensively, with each mile worrying that my car would break down again.

"You feel so good!" I said to Anne, hugging her like my life depended on it when I finally made it home from my ill-fated road trip. Our first embrace when I got home was the best feeling I ever had. I felt like I was coming home not only physically but within my heart and I realized I was ready to make a commitment to Anne. The lease on my apartment was up and I moved in to Anne's apartment and we have been together ever since.

Looking at the *"Journey"* card on our dresser often made me think of this early phase of our relationship. I tried not to romanticize it with too much nostalgia, because it was not an easy time. We had no money, we lived in dilapidated apartments, drove beat up cars which broke down regularly, and worked shitty, dead end jobs. There are many things about this era that I do not miss.

Yet in all the photographs from this era Anne always looks so happy. She was on her own for the first time, striking out into the world and finding her own identity. My favorite photograph shows Anne in front of a restaurant in Chicago called the Fireside Inn, where we had just gone to brunch in the early spring of 1992. The last of the winter snow is melting on the sidewalk, her hair is longer and blonde, before she started coloring it red, and she wears a red, patterned jacket. She has the sweetest smile on her face, looking adorable, and I kept this picture for years on the wall of my art studio. All our problems at the time notwithstanding, it was truly an age of innocence.

Our current situation was anything but an age of innocence. The stress of the move and the war with Lizzie and Wade was threatening to tear us apart. We were at each other's throats to the point where I truly feared that our journey would end in a divorce. We were physically and emotionally exhausted, and we were deeply cynical about the legal system which had failed to protect us. We grimly trudged through each work day in an emotionally numb, vacant stupor. Reflecting on the early years of our relationship made it that much more difficult to confront our current situation, and I wondered how we had found ourselves on such a dark, twisted road. Not only with the dog attack but with our whole journey together we had been through so much, and the thought of letting it all go was heartbreaking.

Although the stress of our lives was pushing us to the breaking point, there was a positive side to the situation, which was that we loved our new house and new neighborhood. We thought our new house was beautiful. It was very similar in size and style to our old house, a brick bungalow style, but it was in much better condition and in a better neighborhood. It had new windows and radiator heat, so it was cozy warm in the winter, while the old house had always been very drafty. We were repainting all the rooms, and Jen had helped us choose the colors. She steered us to neutral colors which would accent our artwork. We painted the living room and dining room a dark blue grey, against which the rich brown and wood hues of my parent's antique furniture and Anne's loom stood out beautifully. I hung up one of my drawings in the dining room, a large pastel of a used car dealership with a bright red sign against green trees in the background, and the colors really popped against our new walls.

We loved our new neighborhood as well. We were a 10 minute walk from a large, beautiful park which had a great Sunday farmers market. We discovered a great restaurant two blocks away, which had been featured on a Chicago restaurant television show called *"Check Please."* There was also a nice bar and grill within walking distance. One of Anne's teaching friends lived in the neighborhood, and we started meeting her for drinks on Friday evenings after work. The waitresses got to know us as regulars, and we tipped them very well, so they filled our wine glasses very full.

We developed a routine where we did any work on the move and the old house on Saturday, and then took Sunday off and stayed home at the new house. When we finished work on Saturday we could not wait to get home to the new house. It felt so good to be there, it was a beautiful sanctuary. Whenever possible, we did not go anywhere on Sunday, staying home at the new house all day, and we really enjoyed the long days in our new home. Even though I was exhausted, I worked hard on painting the walls, because it felt so good to see the new house coming together. The new house made us hopeful, that maybe we could actually move on from this tragedy and start a new life. We sat in the beautiful living room of our new home, looking at each other in amazement, saying to each other, "I can't believe we made it here."

RIPPLE EFFECTS

The dog attack impacted one hundred percent of our lives. From the most important issues down to our recreational activities and hobbies, not one aspect of our lives escaped the ripple effects of the attack. The dog attack was a cancerous tumor on the body of our lives, growing uncontrollably until it infected every cell. It seeped into our lives the way the dust during the Dust Bowl seeped through every windowsill.

One of the major impacts of the attack was on both of our jobs. Anne worked as an art teacher for fifteen years. She taught in schools which had students with a variety of challenges, in some of the toughest neighborhoods in the city. Her students were mostly low income. Her students had a wide range of issues. They came to school with severe disciplinary problems, and Anne had taught students who already had police records. Some children went to school hungry others were victims of home abuse and neglect others suffered from fetal alcohol and drug syndrome. Some students had no running water in the home because of lack of income.

Anne's school was a tough, high stress, often depressing

environment under the best of circumstances. When she developed PTSD symptoms in the wake of the attack, the stress of her job became excruciating and it was very emotionally debilitating for her. She found it increasingly difficult to manage her classes, and to handle the disciplinary issues from her more aggressive students.

"Listen to how loud these kids are!" Anne said to me on the phone one day as she called me from school. She held the phone up to the school hallway and even through the phone I could hear the kids screaming.

"Damn that sounds like wall to wall noise!" I replied when she put the phone back to her ear.

"It is! That's what I listen to every day!" Anne replied. This noisy, aggressive, frenetically high energy environment set off Anne's PTSD symptoms. In one instance she completely lost control of a class, and the students tore up her room, throwing books and turning over tables. She removed herself from the class for the day and refused to teach a second period of the class. She was shaking and crying in the principal's office after the incident. This had never happened prior to the attack, because Anne was a veteran teacher who was very strong with classroom management.

"Today a kid called me the Red Hitler!" Anne told me after work one evening.

"I like that one!" I replied laughing. "I'm gonna have to remember that one for the next time we get into an argument!"

While we found the "Red Hitler" name amusing, many of the names students called Anne and the other teachers were not so funny. Anne had been called "cunt" and "bitch" many times, by children as young as 3rd grade. This made us angry because not only were these verbally abusive names, but also because clearly these children were parroting language they heard from people in their lives. They did not dream this language up on their own.

"If I had given my teachers 10% of the attitude these kids give you my Dad would have just taken me outside and kicked my ass!" I said to Anne many times. "I can't believe the parents tolerate this behavior!" We were consistently upset that such terrible behavior seemed to be accepted by many adult authority figures as part of the norm.

"I'm sorry I don't make more money," I often told Anne. "I wish I could make more so you could just up and quit that hell hole!"

I often felt guilty because Anne made more money than I did and that was part of the reason she felt trapped in such a terrible job. The company I worked for was considering a merger with a larger company, and I was really hoping that a bigger company with deeper pockets would enable me to make more money and give Anne more freedom to make a move to get out.

"If you need to take a job with a pay cut to get out of there, I would support that," I told her several times. "We can find ways to cut back expenses until you find something else."

"I've worked hard for fifteen years to earn the salary I have," Anne replied. "I'm not taking a pay cut!"

When Anne came home on evenings and weekends she was emotionally exhausted. On weekends, she often lacked motivation or energy and would sit in on the couch and watch tv for hours. I was conflicted about this, because I knew how tired she was and wanted her to rest. But I also often got frustrated with her because we had a lot of work to do moving into our new house.

"You have that long Sunday afternoon look on your face," I commented to Anne on many weekends. "Are you worried about going back to work tomorrow?"

Anne nodded, and her facial expression was often anxious and worried on Sunday afternoons, because she was dreading work the next day. She would have anxiety attacks where she had a tense look on her face and shaking hands, which I learned to recognize immediately.

Anne had the opportunity to take a leave of absence from her job, which was approved the school system. I begged her to take the leave of absence, and so did her friends.

"I'll physically bar the door to keep you from going back to that place!" One of Anne's teaching friends told her over dinner at a restaurant one evening. Anne's therapist told her she would approve the leave of absence and provide real reasons and documentation the school needed. But Anne did not take a leave of absence and insisted on soldiering through and continuing to go to work. Neither of us really understood why she resisted taking the leave, and we discussed it at length.

"I want to keep working because I need to prove to myself that I can function as a normal person after the attack," Anne told me, having finally come to that realization after much discussion with both me and her therapist. "I want to know within myself that I can do the same things I did before."

Anne also began to take an on-line real estate class to become a certified real estate agent. She had a good opportunity in real estate, because we had become great friends with Jen our real estate agent, who said she would help mentor Anne once she became certified. The problem was that Anne was so exhausted from her job that she lacked the energy to focus on her real estate class. She missed class deadlines and had to pay extra fees. I wanted her to take her leave of absence and spend that time finishing her real estate class, so she could get into a whole new line of work and escape teaching. But she continued to trudge into her teaching job, coming home with endless stories about abusive students and irresponsible adults. I tried to be supportive, but these stories wore on me and I became frustrated with Anne because I felt she was not doing enough to help herself. Anne was also conflicted about leaving education. While she wanted to get out, she had also invested tremendous time, energy and money into the education profession, and had earned several degrees and certifications. This investment made it hard for her to walk away, no matter how bad it was.

There have been movies made about inner city teaching. In some of these movies the teacher initially struggles to deal with kids from tough backgrounds, but later they find redemption and they bond with their students and make a difference in their community. Anne's job offered no such redemption. The problems of her students were so intractable that no teacher could resolve them.

Worse yet, the political and media attitude toward teachers were often very hostile, blaming the teachers for failing schools. The teachers had gone on strike, the first strike in a generation, and they faced intense criticism in the media, which painted them as being selfish and turning their backs on the children. Many students came to school hungry, abused, neglected, victims of gang violence, but when they mysteriously failed to get Harvard level test scores the teachers got the blame.

Anne had originally gone into inner city teaching with a sense of idealism that education could give these children opportunity and hope, that art could be used as a type of healing. Over 15 years, that idealism had been beaten out of her, replaced by a jaded cynicism, and a bleak and abject feeling of hopelessness.

While Anne's job dealt with some of the lowest income people in Chicago, my job was the opposite because I worked for the most rich and powerful people in the city. I worked for a moving and storage company that specialized in moving fine art, high end furniture, and artifacts. Our typical clients included museums, art galleries, private and corporate art collectors, and affluent auction houses. One of our clients had his name on a wing of an art museum. Another worked as a financial advisor on a presidential election campaign. Our clients owned artwork by Picasso, Cezanne, Jasper Johns and other major artists. They had second homes in high-end resorts. They were wealthy and powerful people, and while they had a wide range of personalities from very nice to very difficult, they all had one thing in common. They were used to getting what they wanted, when they wanted it.

Essentially, my company did the blue collar work for the art world. We built crates for valuable and irreplaceable objects. We loaded the trucks, arranged shipments and security, and moved and installed artwork. We did inventory and collections management, which was my end of the business. I was also a regular forklift driver, moving sculptures and other large artwork which could weigh well over 1,000 pounds.

In the immediate aftermath of the attack, everyone at my workplace was really supportive, and the support was spearheaded by Jeanine, my best friend at work. They had flowers sent to Anne's the hospital room and pitched in to buy her an Amazon gift card for a book to read while she was laid up healing. It was Jeanine who organized all this.

Jeanine was a slim woman in her 30s, with straight shoulder length blonde hair highlighted with pink on the ends. Prior to the attack, she had been a good work buddy, but I did not feel particularly close to her. After the attack, my friendship with her grew tremendously, evolving into a truly beautiful friendship. Jeanine proved to have a heart of gold and also a great sense of humor. She became a friend who I trusted 100%. I confided to her regularly about both workplace and personal issues, and we also shared many good laughs about the various shenanigans in our workplace.

Several months later, I accidentally stumbled upon an email exchange with Jeanine written on the day of the attack. She liked sandwiches from a deli near an off-site storage facility my company owned in Chicago. Early in the afternoon, I emailed my co-workers that I would be spending the afternoon working at the off-site facility, and Jeanine replied asking if I wanted to pick us up subs the deli. I said sure, I'll pick you up a sandwich, and she replied, *"Sweet! Hell yes! I'll take a number 13."*

My email was time stamped at 1:12pm, and she replied at 1:13pm, just about the time Anne was texting Lizzie and going over to her house to meet the dogs. I stopped at the deli and picked up sandwiches for Jeanine and me, then drove to the offsite warehouse and began working on inventory in the storage vault.

This was where I was when I received the screaming, panicked cell phone call from Anne telling me of the attack. It was eerie and haunting to re-read my email correspondence with Jeanine - a lighthearted exchange about a lunch order, written when I was blissfully unaware of the terrible, life changing event that was only minutes away from occurring. Thursday, June 20th had been such an ordinary day, involving storage inventory, a lunch order with a friend, normal things I did all the time. Within minutes, the day devolved into an earthquake which shook our lives to the foundation, and a day that changed our lives forever. Jeanine never got her sandwich, which I ate for dinner that night in the emergency room waiting area at the hospital.

I had a tennis match scheduled after work on the day of the attack. Whenever I played tennis after work, I left my tennis gear bag on the loading dock. The bag was big and cumbersome and more convenient to leave on the dock then drag up to my office. Of course, once the attack took place, my tennis match and bag were forgotten. When I returned to work about a week later, a friend named Andrew had moved my tennis bag up to my office, next to my desk, for safe keeping. It was a small gesture, but I found it meaningful, because it made me feel like people were looking out for us in ways large and small.

One day I was on the phone with a storage client answering some inventory questions he had, when he suddenly asked me about the dog attack and how my wife was doing. I was taken aback when he asked me this, because although I had worked with him for years managing his art collection I had no personal relationship with him. I had no idea that he knew or cared about my personal life. He explained to me that he had gone out to dinner with my boss, who had told him about the attack and everything that was happening in the aftermath. Once I got over my initial surprise, I found his comments to be gracious. As we hung up the phone he said to me, "I truly hope you and your wife achieve justice."

"I had a dream about you and Anne," the general manager of my company told me as we stood around with beers in hand at the office Christmas party. "In my dream, I shot the dogs and then I beat the shit out of their owners!" I thought this dream was remarkable because he had never seen the dogs or met Lizzie and Wade. Throughout the whole experience, I was amazed that people seemed to respond to our situation with real strong emotion. When people offered us support, they were not simply being polite or nice; they seemed to be truly emotional about what had happened to Anne.

A few days before Christmas, I got a nice and compelling email from a friend and former co-worker. I had heard that she got a new job, and I emailed her to say congratulations. She replied with an email that included a heartfelt apology that she had not contacted us in the wake of the dog attack. She wrote, *"I want to offer my sincerest apologies for not reaching out to you after what happened to Anne. I have thought of you two often, and every time I started to write something, the words just didn't seem like enough to show how saddened I was that two of the most genuinely amazing people I know could have something like this happen to them, and all you would have continue to go through, because of it. Please don't feel that my silence meant that I didn't care, it was the exact opposite."*

I completely understood what she was saying. The dog attack saga had been so insane that it was difficult for other people to know what to do or say about it. Both Anne and I totally understood that. Sometimes we did not know what to do or say about it ourselves. So, I appreciated the honesty of my friend's email, and I replied saying I accepted her apology and understood how she felt. How could anyone know how to respond to this situation, which was so twisted and surreal that there was no frame of reference? How could anyone really know what to say?

One day in March a surprise fax was sent to our office. The fax was a petition from the Shipping and Receiving Union, signed by 14 of our employees saying they wanted to unionize. This fax exploded in our office like a bombshell! The 14 signers had not informed much of the rest of the company that they were meeting with the Union, so many of us were completely blindsided. Our general manager was furious and threatened to fire all 14 of the signers. This was illegal and earned him a grievance from the union.

The union debate quickly developed into a civil war within the company. Our crews argued with each other in their trucks. In the offices, people huddled together in corners having hushed, low voiced conversations. Besides the union debate, there was a plan to merge with another company, a larger New York based art moving company which was expanding to Chicago. The specifics of the merger were poorly communicated to the staff by upper management, which added to the climate of tension and confusion. I was strongly in favor of the merger because I thought the new company was exciting, and I also hoped that a bigger company with deeper pockets would pay me a higher salary.

For that reason, I was opposed to unionization, because I was told that the new company would back out of the merger if we became a union shop. I was not anti-union. After all, I was married to a member of the Teachers Union and had strongly supported Anne and the Teachers Union. But I felt that unionization was the wrong approach at the wrong time to resolve the problems of my company.

I also felt, as did the other anti-union people, that the 14 union supporters were not sincere. They were all young, well-educated artists, with left wing political ideals. We felt that they were looking for a political cause and had latched onto the union issue for that purpose and were playing a game of being working class heroes. I felt that this was disrespectful to the long history of the labor movement, where many courageous people risked their lives to campaign for workers' rights. One of my colleagues said it best when he called them "champagne socialists."

The union issue would be decided by a company vote, and only crew people were allowed a vote. Upper level management was not allowed to vote. I was in the eye of the storm of the union debate, because my job description existed on an ambiguous borderline between management and crew. The Labor Alliance Board (LAB) ruled that I was eligible to vote, and the union supporters were outraged. They felt that I was a senior manager who was a company mole who had been planted into the vote to skew the result against them. I tried to explain that I had no control over my eligibility, that it was determined by the company and union attorneys, but they did not buy it and expressed major resentment toward me.

During this, Anne and I were in the midst of the move from hell, and this sudden and dramatic increase in workplace tension was the last thing I needed. I felt that I had a target on my back from the war with Lizzie and Wade, and now I was a target at work because the union supporters hated me. Suddenly, I felt targeted everywhere. My tennis bag which I used to leave on the loading dock I moved next to my desk for safekeeping. I had some of my own artworks in company storage, and I moved them to an offsite storage facility where the union supporters did not have access. I found myself doing the same type of things to protect myself at work that I did in the terrible neighborhood situation. I constantly felt a dark sense of tension. The support and goodwill I received in the immediate aftermath of the attack had evaporated to be replaced by a feeling that I was working in a snake pit of liars and backstabbers.

I always carried pepper spray on my trips to the old house, but I normally did not carry it anywhere else and left it in my car. One day I went into work forgetting that my pepper spray canister was in my pocket. I absent mindedly took it out of my pocket and set it on the edge of my desk.

"Damn Will! Are you packing heat!?" One of my coworkers exclaimed when he saw the canister on the edge of my desk. "I'll be sure not to piss you off today!"

Throughout my employment history, I had a reputation as a laid back guy, but during the war with Lizzie and Wade my work persona became significantly more edgy and intense, and it played into my response to the union debate.

One day during the union debate, a coworker named Aaron confronted me about my attitude saying, "It's really difficult to listen to you rant about the union issue every single morning!"

"Tell Aaron I said thank you!" Anne said when I told her about the incident. "I've been trying to tell you for months that you've gotten too intense!" I did relay her message to Aaron, saying to him, "I appreciate you being honest with me about being too intense. My wife's been trying to tell me the same thing."

One day I checked my mail when I got home, and I saw that the union had sent a recruitment letter to my house. I was surprised because I had no idea that the union had my home address, and I had not authorized anyone to give it to them. This upset me because I was in a hyper vigilant security mindset because of the war with Lizzie and Wade, and I did not trust the union.

"Why is the Union sending letters to my house?!" I complained loudly and bitterly in the weekly company staff meeting. "That's a violation! I never authorized anyone to give them my address! I don't want these people to know where I live!"

Unfortunately, nothing could be done about it. It was a requirement of the LAB that all eligible voters had to have their contact information provided to the union. I was not at all happy about this rule!

The specter of potential workplace intimidation was very real to me. Besides the ongoing intimidation from Lizzie and Wade, I had witnessed an incident, years earlier at a different job. A manager had an argument with another worker, and when he left work at the end of the day he found that his car had all four tires slashed.

"I feel like people are thinking I'm going crazy!" I said to Jeanine. "But workplace intimidation is real! I've seen it!" Although nobody said it to me directly, I sensed that my coworkers were beginning to think I was going over the edge mentally, that I had watched too many gangster movies about Jimmy Hoffa. It was an example of how Anne and I were living in an alternative reality, which people living more normal lives could not understand.

Besides being outspoken about notifying authorities in the dog case, I was similarly outspoken during the bitter union debate. Our company had frequent meetings regarding both the union and the merger and I was one of the most vocal people in these meetings, so much so that before the union vote the company attorneys approached my boss and asked him to tell me to tone it down.

"Legally, I can't order you not to talk about the union," my boss told me when he had called me into his office. "But if you would tone it down somewhat, I would appreciate it."

"Sure, that's fine," I replied. "I've said everything I had to say about it already, so anything I say now would just be repeating myself."

"The company attorneys had a meeting with our boss about me," I told Jeanine later. "They basically asked him to tell me to shut up!"

"Oh my God! That's hilarious!" Jeanine exclaimed, laughing loudly. "You rabble rouser you!"

I formed a partnership with Jeanine and another coworker named Leslie, and together we organized a campaign with the union no voters. We arranged a meeting with the other no and undecided voters, and together we drafted a statement of eight reasons why we were opposed to unionization. We posted the statement by the time clock, as well as in the conference room and break room. We tried to make this a positive dialogue with the union yes voters, but they were not having it and it made them hate me even more, which increased my sense of feeling targeted.

The union no vote won 14 to 13, but the election was contested because of union grievances, and it went to a hearing of the LAB to decide the outcome. I did not attend the hearing, but afterward the general manager warned me that a union supporter named Milos had said extremely negative things about me in his testimony. I was surprised because I liked Milos and thought we had a good working relationship.

Before confronting the issue, I wanted to see for myself what he said, and I requested and received a copy of the hearing transcript. When I read Milos's testimony, I was shocked at the malicious lies he told about me. He testified that I was a verbally abusive supervisor who flew into violent, shaking rages, and that I had been unsafe when I drove the forklift moving a large sculpture by Jeff Koons. I was completely blindsided. Milos and had I talked openly about many workplace issues, which I had thought was a positive dialogue, and I had advocated to upper management that he get a promotion. I had no idea he hated me to the point of lying under oath about me.

On a Friday morning, I confronted Milos about his lies in the union hearing, and I wanted to do so in a cold, professional manner. We were in his office, an open office space with partitions. I was planning to be direct, brutally honest, without losing my cool, but once I started talking, I lost my temper and started yelling at him.

"I read your testimony at the union hearing, and I actually laughed! I'm circulating it among my family and friends as a running joke!" Milos was seated at his desk with his back to me. He said nothing, but I saw the muscles of his shoulders twitch and his shoulders hunch up toward his neck.

"Yesterday I called my attorney and made an inquiry about suing you!" I continued, my voice becoming more loud and angry with every word. "If you file a union grievance against me I'll file a lawsuit against you for perjury, slander, and defamation of character!"

The previous evening, I had shown Anne a transcript of the union hearing, and when she read it she was so angry she wanted to come into my workplace and confront Milos herself. Anne and I had strong protective feelings toward each other. I had often wanted to march into her principal's office to give him a piece of my mind about how she was treated in his school. Now it was Anne's turn, and she wanted to come into my workplace to defend me.

"My wife read your lying testimony and she's so pissed off, she wants to come in here and confront you herself!" I shouted at Milos. "It's not gonna go well for you because she's a whole lot tougher than I am! My wife's gonna come in here and kick your ass!"

"I learned how to play hardball during the dog attack!" Was the last thing I yelled at Milos. "Don't play with me, boy!" I put special emphasis on the last word boy, and I then walked away from him and went outside to cool down.

Later, when the smoke cleared from the incident, Anne and I found it hilarious that I had threatened Milos that she would kick his ass. She shared the story with a couple of her girlfriends who also found it hilarious. I felt that I had made history because I had to be the only man in the history of American labor to use his wife to threaten a coworker.

In that moment, however, nothing was funny. As my anger dissipated, I began to worry that I had gone over the line and gotten myself in trouble. Would I get fired? Would Milos call the police on me?

"I'm scared!" Anne said when I called her and told her about the confrontation. "Are you going to get in trouble?!" I had inventory work to do at an offsite storage warehouse, which was a good excuse to get away from the main offices and cool off by myself. In the end I did not get fired, but I did receive a written warning for threatening and verbally abusive behavior toward a coworker. It was the only time in my 30 year work history that I had ever received disciplinary action for personal misbehavior with a coworker.

Later in the afternoon, I began to feel remorse and embarrassment. I had no apologies for Milos, who completely deserved everything I yelled at him, but I was remorseful that my behavior had been so unprofessional. I sent an apology email to everyone who could have potentially been within earshot.

"Can I talk to you, please?" I asked Jeanine, walking into her office late in the day, my voice low and quiet, my eyes misting with tears. I felt humble in that moment, imploring my friend that I needed her help. Jeanine was a smoker, and often when she stepped outside for her cigarette break, I would go with her so we could talk privately about all the issues in our workplace. She could see that I was upset, and quickly fished her cigarettes and lighter out of her purse and we walked outside.

"I'm afraid I really fucked up when I yelled at Milos!" I said to Jeanine as soon as we stepped out onto the sidewalk, my voice breaking, fighting back tears. Jeanine put her hand on my shoulder to comfort me. She did not say much and mainly just listened as I told her about the incident, which was something she was very good at. She was my workplace confidante, and I often worried that our friendship was wearing on her, because I was constantly asking her to step outside with me to discuss some drama at our job. All our workplace conflict was stressful and exhausting, piled on top of the already excruciating stress of the war with Lizzie and Wade. At work, Jeanine was the only thing standing between me and a nervous breakdown.

Upon reflection, I began to see disturbing parallels between the union fight and the legal battle with Lizzie and Wade. In both cases, we witnessed somebody shamelessly lie under oath in a legal proceeding. In both cases, we had someone who we supported maliciously turn against us. Anne had gone over to Lizzie's house to do her a favor and was repaid with a vicious dog attack and threats, lies and abuse. I had advocated to upper management that Milos get a promotion, saying he was potentially the best warehouse coordinator we ever had, and I was repaid by him maliciously stabbing me in the back. Twice in a year, I had been a victim of a crime, this time libel and slander, and both times the criminal went unpunished. In contrast, I had been punished, getting a written warning for yelling at Milos when it was he who had committed the crime. I began to think that the legal system did a much better job of punishing victims than criminals.

"How can this be happening!?" I asked myself in consternation. *"What is going on that there is so much hostility in my life!?"*

I could not understand why, suddenly, I seemed to be making enemies everywhere I went. I viewed myself in general as an easy-going guy who mostly got along with people. Over 25 years ago, I had a couple bitter breakups with old girlfriends, who probably hated me if they still even gave me a second thought. Other than that, I could not think of anyone who had serious animosity toward me. For the second time in a year, I was mixed up with people who had no integrity or conscience. Anne and I had both made serious mistakes in character judgment, her with Lizzie and me with Milos.

In different ways, both my workplace and Anne's had become emotionally toxic, and our workplace issues played into the dog attack issues in very negative ways. The toxic environment of both our jobs had become an impediment to our efforts to heal and move on. Anne often thought that my job had terrible timing, because my job problems tended to happen during unfortunate times in our personal life.

Anne was right. My confrontation with Milos was on June 13th, which was our wedding anniversary. After work, Anne and I had reservations at our favorite neighborhood restaurant. The waiter seated us outside on a lovely patio, on a beautiful June evening with slanting sunlight splashing across our table. I tried my best to put the events of the workday out of my mind to enjoy our romantic evening, but I could not shake it, and I was tense and distracted throughout our dinner. Anne tried to be patient with me because she knew what a rough day I had, but as my mood did not improve, she became frustrated that it was ruining our romantic dinner. Eventually she snapped at me, "Your goddamned job sure has bad timing!"

THROUGH THE LOOKING GLASS

"I find it amazing that you do not seem bitter," Anne's therapist remarked to her in one of their sessions. "You are still such an open and generous person."

One of my friends made a similar comment to me, texting, *"It amazes and humbles me that you have faced all that in such a short span of time, and you are still such a wonderful, caring person."*

I believe that there is a one-word explanation, and that one word is love. There are times when beautiful things come out of terrible events, and one of the beautiful things that developed from the horror of the dog attack was the tremendous outpouring of support we received from our family and friends, and people from all aspects of our lives. We made some wonderful new friends through the dog attack, and became closer with existing friends. Our love for one another became deeper and richer as well. The love and support we received in the aftermath of the attack was amazing, for which we will be eternally grateful.

While the support we received in the immediate aftermath was tremendous, several months after the attack, our friends and family began to move on to other issues. This was understandable because Anne was back at work living superficially a normal life and we had moved away from the evil neighbors, so people thought the dog attack and its effects were over with. This was not the case at all, because we continued to deal with issues related to the attack into the present day. Both Anne's physical scarring and emotional PTSD are long term issues which we will continue to deal with for months and years, and quite possibly for the rest of our lives.

Anne's mother once made a profound comment, saying that the hardest part about losing her husband was the several months after the funeral. Her family and friends had returned home and gone back to their lives, the cards and flowers had stopped pouring in, and she was left alone with her loss. Several months after the attack, we felt much the same way, isolated and alone on an island. It was no one's fault, and we knew our family and friends still cared about us, but it was just in the nature of how a tragedy plays out.

This sense of isolation created a feeling of alienation which I struggled with in the aftermath of the dog attack. The whole situation had become so crazy, twisted, and psychotic that I felt like I had gone through the looking glass into a new surreal alternative reality, completely disconnected from normal life. These feelings started to intensify as things began to calm down from the dog attack crisis, which gave us more time to reflect on the horror in the details of what happened. In some ways, this phase became more challenging, because during the crisis, we focused all our energy on responding to the latest crazy development and trying to survive it. As events began to calm down, we no longer had that automatic, immediate focus and we began to think about the big picture, how the dog attack had impacted the larger context of our lives.

For several months, the dog attack and the war with Lizzie and Wade had defined our lives, but as we began to move on, we did not know what defined us. I looked at Anne, or looked at myself in the mirror, and felt like I was looking at a stranger. I felt lost because I had become another person, but I did not know him. We had moved into a new place, but I could not find it. Anne had become a new person, but I did not recognize her. I felt locked into an alternative reality as though I was walking through a strange landscape I had never seen before.

I began to understand that Anne and I could never return to normal as it once was. We might eventually find a new normal, but we would never return to the life we had lived in the past. We would have to create our new reality from the beginning. We felt like we could see normal reality as if through a pane of glass, where we could observe it but were not actually present.

One cold, bright sunlit day in February, I walked down the street to my job, the same place where I had worked for fifteen years, and it felt like a place I had never seen before. I cut through the loading dock on the way to my office, observing normal scenes of our crews loading their trucks. I saw our crews pushing crates and heard the usual clanging of lift gates and pallet jacks, the roar of the forklift motor, but I experienced these everyday sights and sounds as if through a prism or glass pane where I was removed. I could see normal reality but was no longer a part of it, because I had become part of a twisted, parallel reality.

It did not help that the dog attack saga was so strange that we had no frame of reference. We had been through other experiences which were painful and challenging, but there was a common ground with other people who have gone through the same thing. When both my parents passed away, it was a landslide event which shook my life to the foundation. But as hard as it was, there are many people who have lost a parent or another beloved older relative, so our experience was not unique. Many other people could relate to it. The same applied to our miscarriages and fertility problems, many couples have struggled with fertility issues.

But with the dog attack, it was different, because we had never heard of anyone who was mauled by two vicious dogs and then had a subsequent war with criminal dog owners. Anne and I often felt out there alone on an island, as if nobody could understand us, though it was not anybody's fault. The dog attack and its aftermath were just so horrible and surreal that nobody could wrap their brain around it.

I struggled to find words to define this strange feeling of alienation from my own life, which I had never experienced before. At times I felt like I was watching a movie of my life, with someone who looked like me playing a lead role, but I was not actually living this life myself. One night, I was watching TV alone late at night after Anne had gone to bed, and I found a re-run of the movie *"Thelma and Louise."* I had seen the movie before and always liked it, so I watched it again. It features two blue collar women on a road trip vacation, which takes a dark turn when a man tries to rape Thelma in the parking lot of a honky-tonk bar and Louise blows him away with a gun. They have no confidence that the criminal justice system will be fair to them, so instead of calling the police they take off on a crazy, desperate run to Mexico.

"Something's crossed over in me and I can't go back!" Thelma says to Louise near the end of the movie.

"That's it!" I exclaimed out loud to myself when I heard the line, jumping up and pointing at the TV screen. *"That's what I feel like!"*

That line hit me like a ton of bricks! In my previous viewings of the movie I had never even noticed it, yet it summed up perfectly my feelings of alienation. It was such a simple line, only ten words and one sentence, and yet it completely defined my struggle to delineate my strange new reality.

"Something's crossed over in me and I can't go back!"

It was that simple.

I identified with *"Thelma and Louise"* on a whole new level when I watched it for the first time after the dog attack. While I have always been a fan of the movie, I saw it in a new way. Thelma and Louise were like Anne and me because they had been living normal lives, had become victims of a crime, and in the aftermath of the crime, their lives had turned bat shit crazy. I really identified with their desperation as they ran from the law on their wild road trip through the Desert Southwest. Our move felt like their road trip, a crazy desperate run to escape from a bad situation. The movie ends with Thelma and Louise driving off the rim of the Grand Canyon to escape from the police. I am happy to say that my story with Anne did not end that way, but there were certainly moments where we seemed to be headed in that direction. I had tears in my eyes as I watched the movie.

Anne changed dramatically in the months after the dog attack, both physically and emotionally. Initially, there was an extreme decrease in her appetite after the attack. I did research on-line, trying to find the best foods to facilitate healing, but Anne was not hungry, and ate very little of what I served her. Initially I was worried, but we spoke to her doctor who said she was not concerned as long as Anne was eating when she was hungry, and eating good quality foods. I came to realize that Anne would eat what she wanted, at the time she wanted it, and that was the right thing. I did not need to push her to eat more than she wanted.

Anne always had food issues dating back to her adolescence, and clearly the dog attack had re-kindled these issues which led to her loss of appetite. She had been through bulimia as a teenager, and she had stopped that on her own, but the dog attack seemed to re-kindle her need to control events through food, and she ate very little.

Both the physical and psychological changes in Anne were difficult for me to process. She lost 25-30 pounds in the months after the dog attack, and I really struggled to deal with the dramatic changes in her appearance and behavior. Her face and neck became thinner, her body more angular. Prior to the attack, Anne had a curvy, voluptuous body, which I always admired, but afterward she appeared much smaller than she did before the attack. Anne was happy with her weight loss, because she perpetually worried that she was overweight and had always wanted to be skinny. I was not so happy about it because I missed her curves, and I also felt like I did not know this strange new woman who was my wife. At times, Anne appeared almost ghostly to me, like an apparition of the woman I knew before the attack. Her face became gaunt and pale, with haunted eyes, as though the real Anne was buried somewhere deep inside, unable to communicate with me on the outside.

Anne's body language and gestures changed after the attack,

becoming more abrupt and jerky, as if she was always on edge about something. We started to call this *"blade hands"* because she would wave her hands flat in a circular motion with her fingers straight out.

"My 3rd grade girls are starting to imitate my hand gestures," Anne told me one day after teaching, mimicking her own gestures.

"Cool! You're teaching them your blade hands!" I replied.

Anne's overall energy level decreased dramatically. She started to go to bed early every night, often falling asleep in bed around 8pm. This disrupted her sleep patterns and she would often wake up around 2-3am and stay awake the rest of the night. This would make her so tired that she would fall asleep even earlier the next night and it became a vicious cycle. She became more stressed out and irritable, always on edge, and reacted strongly to even the most minor mistake or problem that developed. And there were physical scars, the deep rings around both thighs, and on her arms, shoulders and neck, that dramatically changed Anne's appearance. The scars also caused her long-term pain, which varied depending on weather conditions and environment.

Anne and I both sought counseling in the aftermath of the attack, and Anne was diagnosed with post traumatic stress disorder (PTSD). We had no prior knowledge of PTSD other than hearing news reports about military veterans returning from Iraq or Afghanistan with it, and it was a major adjustment for both us learning to recognize and respond to her PTSD symptoms.

Anne developed a distinctive facial expression related to her PTSD symptoms, which she never had before the attack. At times her upper lip would twitch and curl, and whenever that happened, I knew that she was experiencing some symptom of PTSD. Often, she had this expression late at night when she was tired, right before going to bed.

For Anne's birthday, we attended a performance of the opera *Madame Butterfly* at the Lyric Opera House in Chicago. During intermission, we stood in the densely packed lobby which was a huge space with ornate decorations and extremely high ceilings, a tall stairway leading to a second-floor balcony, and a thick crowd of well-dressed people milling around.

"Can we go back into theater?" Anne asked me. "It's dark and it feels safer."

"I'm feeling a panic attack coming on!" Anne continued, speaking low into my ear. "All these people seem huge, like they are giants towering over me. I feel really small." We went back into theater, where Anne felt safer because it was darker and our seats were in a more enclosed space, where there were not seemingly huge people milling around her.

Anne had a similar PTSD episode one Saturday morning when we were shopping at Costco. I left her so I could go to the restroom and when I returned, she seemed to be on the verge of a panic attack.

"What's wrong, Honey?!" I asked as I saw her clinging to our shopping cart, with white knuckles and a pale, frightened expression on her face.

"This place is too much!" Anne replied. "There's just so much going on!" The Costco environment had set off her PTSD, because it was crowded with many people shopping. The visual environment caused her sensory overload with product labeling in many different colors, shapes and sizes, glaring fluorescent lighting, and crowds of people pushing shopping carts loaded with items.

"Just go back out to the car if you want," I told her. "I can finish checking out and meet you out there."

"No, I'll stay here, I have to learn to deal with this," Anne replied, taking deep breaths as we stood in the checkout line. Although Costco is a much different physical space than the Lyric Opera House, both places set off Anne's PTSD in a similar way. Both have large interiors with high ceilings, a lot of people moving around, and an extremely high level of visual stimulation, which seemed to trigger Anne's PTSD in a negative way.

All these changes in Anne made me feel like I was married to a stranger and these feelings were exacerbated by the fact that I myself had also changed dramatically. I too had lost weight from the physical work of the move, losing ten pounds during those months despite eating like a horse. I also experienced major emotional changes. I am generally a pretty laid-back guy under normal circumstances, but after the attack, I developed a darker and more intense persona, constantly on edge. I carried a deep well of anger in the aftermath of the dog attack which I did not know how to process. I had literally become lean and mean. A lyric from folk songwriter Townes Van Zandt spoke to me of my new persona, *"Now you wear your skin like iron, and your breath's as hard as kerosene."*

"Can you stop swearing so much?!" Anne asked me one day. "I have to listen to that language all day at school and it's wearing to hear it all the time at home as well!"

Anne was right that my language had become laced with profanities, no matter what I was talking about. I was bitter about the way we had been treated in this case, by both the legal system and the news media, and it was a challenge to process this intense feeling of injustice. I began to research people who had been victims of a major legal injustice in an effort to understand how they dealt with it.

I was grateful that my mother was not alive to know about the dog attack. Of course she would have been extremely upset, and never would have understood the evil, ugly behavior of Lizzie and Wade. My mother was an old fashioned, traditional, Victorian lady with a demure disposition and impeccable moral character. Throughout her life, she maintained a sense of naïve innocence. She was so pure in her heart and soul that she had no understanding of the dark side of human nature, so Lizzie and Wade would have been incomprehensible to her.

My Father was the opposite and there were many times during the dog attack crisis when I wished he was alive. If the attack had happened when he was alive, in his prime, he would have had a towering rage, and he would have gone after the dog owners by any means necessary. Once when I was a boy, we were in the lobby of a seedy hotel in Denver, Colorado, and a strange man gave me some change and told me to buy him a pack of cigarettes from a vending machine across the room. My Father shoved the change back in his hand, growling at him, *"Get your own God damned cigarettes!"* During the attack crisis I often wished we could take shelter behind my father's protective anger.

Anne's father also would have protected us, but in a different way. He grew up dirt poor in West Virginia and through hard work and smart financial decisions, became a successful business executive who provided a comfortable life for his family. He was meticulous in everything he did. He would have methodically studied our legal case from every angle to make sure we got the best legal representation possible. We would have loved to have him in the room when we met with our attorneys, because he would have asked all the right questions. Anne had thought of her Father during the attack. Strangely she had heard birds chirping around her head, and she came to believe that it represented the spirits of her late Father and Grandfather, who had rushed in to protect her.

When Lizzie and Wade started their attempts to intimidate Anne and me, it brought back some personal demons from my distant past. When I was in 7th and 8th grade I was the victim of severe bullying. I was a small, scrawny, awkward boy, an easy target. I was punched in the face and stomach, kneed in the groin, and I had a case of severe acne, which was fuel for verbal abuse. One kid used to call me pizza face because of my complexion.

I rarely if ever told my parents, teachers, or any other adult authority figure about the bullying. I thought I was a sissy for getting bullied and telling an adult would make me that much more of a sissy. It was also the mid-1970s and there was none of the dialogue about bullying that exists today. The prevailing attitude was that boys will be boys. So, I suffered in silence, and never spoke about my bullying until many years into my adulthood.

The war with Lizzie and Wade awakened echoes from my bullying era. For the first time in 35 years, I consistently felt afraid for my physical safety. I had forgotten what it feels like to be in constant physical fear. In 8th grade I was afraid to drink out of the school drinking fountain, because my head would be down, and I felt vulnerable to getting hit. Many years later, I watched a wildlife program on TV showing a watering hole in Africa which the animals approached with extreme caution because of the danger of lurking predators. I realized that this was the same mentality I had with the school drinking fountain, that during my bullying era I had lived with the mindset of a vulnerable wild animal.

I felt that same fear on every trip I made to the old house, gnawing at the pit of my stomach every time I went in our front door. The difference was that this time I was determined to speak out against the abuse from Lizzie and Wade. I was resolute in my efforts to seek justice despite their attempts to intimidate us. As a 12 year old boy, I never told any adult authority about the abuse I suffered. As a 50 year old man, I told any authority figure who would listen and I was extremely outspoken.

Of course, my main motivation for being so outspoken was to protect Anne and myself, and to bring Lizzie and Wade to justice. But on a deeper level, I also did it for my inner 12 year old boy who had been bullied and never spoke out. I did not understand this at the time, but only realized it months later when I had time to think it through. By standing up to the attempted intimidation from Lizzie and Wade, and being very outspoken about notifying the authorities, I felt like I was vindicating my inner 12 year old boy who had never had a voice. In a very twisted way, the dog attack forced me to confront the long buried pain, anger, and humiliation from my bullying era, and to come to terms with it.

I had several disturbing dreams about the dogs, all with very similar themes. Most occurred when we were still living at the old house next to the dogs and their owners, and they became less frequent as we moved and I spent less time there. Clearly, the old house triggered the dog dreams, because whenever I had to go back there for any length of time they would reoccur.

In one of my dreams, I found the vicious dogs sleeping on our bed. Anne was in the house, and for some reason it was crowded with a lot of other people as well. I was rushing around as quietly as possible, trying to get everyone out of the house before the dogs woke up and attacked.

In another, I found the dogs in the yard in my childhood home in Colorado. My elderly mother was in the yard, and I was trying to push her into the house before the dogs attacked, and she was moving too slow because of her age.

Yet another dream featured the dogs trying to break through a gap in our wood fence, and I was frantically trying to nail a board in place before they broke through.

In my last dream, I had to retrieve something we had left in Lizzie and Wade's house. Oddly enough, it was a trivial object, some sort of board game like Scrabble or Monopoly. I had to go through the house and yard to get to the shed where the objects were kept. One of the dogs was in the shed, along with a little girl in charge of the dog. I was quietly trying to get the board game off a shelf without provoking the dog to attack me. I had no idea who the little girl was, but Anne thought that the girl represented her. All these dreams expressed an extreme sense of vulnerability, where the dogs had invaded the personal space of me and my family, and I was desperately trying to protect someone from them.

One night in our new house, we had an innocent domestic incident which triggered a nightmare for Anne. She was asleep in bed, and one of our dogs, Alice, was sleeping on the floor at the end of the bed. Alice had black fur, and was sleeping in a shadow cast by the bed, so I did not see her and tripped over her when I walked into the bedroom. This startled Alice and woke her up, and she tried to jump on the bed, twice mis-timing her jump and falling back on the floor. This in turn woke Anne up, and she was also startled and frightened hearing Alice trying to jump on the bed. Anne sat up and frantically pushed herself back with her arms, up against the wall of the bedroom, the same position she had pushed herself back in during the dog attack. Later that night, she fell asleep and had a nightmare about an attack, the first nightmare since the attack. The nightmare featured Anne in a field, being attacked by huge cats with long fangs like those of a saber toothed tiger. She crossed hands in front of her face to defend herself, then woke up terrified, and did not want to tell me.

Each year, we spent Thanksgiving at the home of Anne's sister Amy in Grosse Pointe Michigan, an upscale suburb of Detroit with tree lined streets and large, stately brick homes. Amy's Thanksgiving dinner table was always elegant, set with fine china and crystal sparkling from candlelight. Anne's family had a tradition where we went around the table and everyone took turns saying what they were thankful for in the past year.

"I'm thankful that Anne is alive!" I said when it was my turn to speak. "We came awfully close to losing her!" Amy got Anne a beautiful card, which she purchased during the dog attack crisis, but then forgot to send it and gave it to Anne over two years later. It was no less meaningful to Anne for the delay. The front of the card was about overcoming adversity, and next to the inside caption Amy wrote *"this still applies."* The inside caption read, *"Your courage is inspiring!"*

On Memorial Day weekend, we visited Anne's mother. We did this every year, and we always did a lot of yard work for her Mother. We refreshed the mulch around her trees cleaned her gutters, and Anne always trimmed her hedges with an electric trimmer. As Anne was trimming, I noticed that she seemed to be favoring her right arm as though it was hurting her.

"What's wrong? Is your elbow scar bothering you?" I asked. "I can finish the trimming if you need me to."

"I think I'll take you up on that," Anne replied, wincing as she set the trimmer down on the grass. Anne suffered long term pain from her scars, and one on her right elbow bothered her. Ironically, this was one of the smallest scars, barely visible looking more like a kitchen grease burn. It was the location that bothered her, because the dog bite had hit her right on her elbow tendon.

One Sunday morning, I heard an interesting television interview with a woman who was the subject of a famous Vietnam War photograph showing a naked little girl running screaming from a napalm attack. She had major long-term pain from her burn scars, and as she grew up as a young woman she worried that the scars made her too ugly to ever find love. Fortunately, that was not the case and she ended up happily married. I told Anne about this interview and she began to research how this woman had dealt with the long-term pain of her scars.

Anne did not talk much about the pain from her scars. This was remarkable because she was always very open with me about discussing physical problems - migraine headaches, period issues, head colds. But she talked very little about the pain from the dog attack scars, and I knew it was because her emotional pain matched her physical pain.

During this visit, we stayed in Anne's childhood bedroom, and she showed me artifacts from her childhood. She loved animals as a girl, and she showed me Beatrix Potter books which she read over and over, illustrated with wonderful pen and ink drawings of the various animal characters. She showed me a small glass case which contained tiny toy animals, such as a pewter giraffe about one inch tall. Anne described how her mother's friends were always amazed that she could play by herself for hours quietly, needing little supervision. Looking at all of Anne's toys and books, I could feel the spirit of her as an innocent little girl, happily playing with her toy animals, absorbed in her Beatrix Potter books, living in world where everyone was nice, living in a world where there were no scars.

THE SCAR DANCE

"Friday June 20th is the year anniversary of the dog attack. We are having a party on Saturday June 21st and you are invited! Our party is a celebration of our survival of the dog attack and its horrible aftermath, and is also a housewarming party for our new home, a summer solstice party, and an opportunity to say thank you to the many people who have supported us throughout this long, dark journey."

This was the text of a party evite we sent to family and friends, which we named *"Coming into the Light."* It was a big effort for us to have this party, because we had recently moved into the new house and were still working hard to get the old house ready to rent. Plus, we had not entertained in a long time in any big way, because our old house was always under construction. During the week before the party, we seriously considered cancelling it, because we started to think it was just too much for us in the overall context of things. But we pushed hard to get the new house ready, painting, cleaning, organizing, because we knew the party felt so right and would be worth the effort in the end. We were right to push through because the party was beautiful, and totally worth every ounce of sweat and stress we put into preparing for it.

Besides inviting family and friends, we decided to invite Maureen from the alderman's office. We did not have a personal relationship with her, but we felt it was appropriate because she had been a great source of support. She replied with the following email which we found very meaningful. *"Drummond & Anne - thank you so much for the invite to your party tomorrow! I hope it is a day of celebration for you after a very traumatic year. Your strength and resilience is very inspiring. Unfortunately, I will be out of town, but I wish you all the best and please stay in touch."*

It was a beautiful night and the party came off just the way we hoped it would, with just the right group of friends from all aspects of both our lives. One thing I found heartwarming about our party was that all our different friends were talking to each other. People who had never met each other before were talking openly and at length, and it gave the party a terrific energy.

Our party was an outdoor barbeque, and there was a heavy thunderstorm in the middle of the evening, but it did not dampen the festivities. All our friends came inside, and crowded onto our back porch eating, drinking, talking, and watching the storm which seemed somehow appropriate, as if the pelting rain was washing away the hardship and pain of the past year, washing us clean to begin our lives anew. After an hour, the storm blew over, and the sun came back out. We all went back outside in our yard, and the fresh raindrops sparkled in the evening sun.

The party on June 21st felt like day one of our healing and moving on from the dog attack. Prior to June 21st we had done virtually no healing, because until recently every aspect of the dog attack was still in play. We just settled our lawsuit in the spring, and we just finished our work on the old house the week before the party. Our last call-the-police incident with Lizzie and Wade was within the last month. Therefore, it had been difficult if not impossible to move on from the dog attack in any meaningful way, because the dog attack had not actually ended in any meaningful way. The party was meant as a celebration of Anne and I finally beginning our healing, and emerging out of our long, dark tunnel of pain and sorrow into our beautiful new life.

Ever since spring and summer came, Anne had been feeling self-conscious about showing her scars. During the winter it was a non-issue, because everyone was bundled up against the brutal Chicago winter and exposing as little skin as possible. But as the warmer weather came around, Anne was concerned about whether she could wear tank tops, shorts, swim suits, and the like, and she was worried about what she could wear during the warm months.

The party had a poignant moment which dealt with the issue of the scars and symbolized the beginning of our healing. At the end of the party, everyone had left except for Jen and her partner Jim, who stayed to help us clean up. As Jen was doing dishes, she pulled Anne up from her chair and they started dancing together in the kitchen to a Blues song on the radio.

"Let's see your scars!" Jen yelled across the room to Anne. "Pull your dress up, let's see your scars!" Anne was wearing a very pretty, navy blue dress with a vintage feel to it, and she pulled her dress up to her hips to reveal the deep ring of scars on both thighs. The two women swayed around the kitchen dancing a swanky, bluesy dance. Anne held her dress up to reveal her scars, which were a pale chalky white color, lighter than her natural skin, pulling her skin taught between them.

It was beautiful to watch this dance. It was as if Anne was reclaiming her body and her spirit from the dog attack. The dance had a primal quality to it, as though she was summoning ancient healing spirits, and I had tears in my eyes watching them. Beginning that moment, I have referred to it in my mind as The Scar Dance.

"You're gorgeous!" Jen kept yelling to Anne across the room. "You're God-damned gorgeous!"

We followed up the party with a road trip vacation out West. We had not taken this type of vacation in years, but we wanted it this year because it felt right to just get in the car and go, with no itinerary or reservations, just the freedom to spontaneously explore anywhere we wanted. We just loaded our camping gear and our dogs in the van and headed West, with no specific idea of where we were going. The West seemed like the right destination because we wanted to find remote, wide open spaces, where we could feel far away from the excruciating stresses of the past year.

The American West is also where I grew up. I had not been out there in years, because I know the region well from my childhood, and I was more interested in exploring other areas of the country I have never seen. But this year, given everything that had happened, it seemed appropriate to go back out West, to go home and get back to my roots. Anne loves the West as well. She does not have the background there that I do, but she had really enjoyed previous trips we took out there.

The American West is a vast landscape, and although I explored it extensively in my youth, there are still huge regions I have never seen. Northern Wyoming is one of those regions, and it is a spectacular, majestic landscape, with high plains and foothills that lead into the Rocky Mountains. The landscape can be intimidating, with huge dramatic skies that are constantly changing, towering black storm clouds and violent thunderstorms that can come out of nowhere.

At the foothills of the Rocky Mountains in Northern Wyoming, we drove through Thunder Basin National Grassland, the only car on a narrow two-lane highway, our cell phones turned off in our glove compartment because they were out of range. The endless expanse of tall, dry, windswept grass enveloped me like an embrace from my father as a young boy. The bright blue sky and dazzling clear sunlight spoke to me of long summer days in my childhood. The winding highway led me back to long school bus rides to high school track meets, listening to Lynyrd Skynyrd, the Cars and Fleetwood Mac on an 8 track tape player. The strength of my spirit felt renewed by the rugged beauty of this landscape, and my soul basked in the boundless freedom of its silent desolation.

After we left Thunder Basin, we found our way to Crazy Woman Canyon, a beautiful place to camp. Rugged, sand colored rock walls jutted upward on both sides of us. Delicate purple wildflowers carpeted the floor of the canyon, and a rapid stream flowed through the middle of the canyon, flowing across dark green moss-covered rocks. We returned from a morning hike up a steep dirt road which led into the canyon, winded and thirsty from the dry, crisp mountain air. Our dogs, Pandora and Alice, were panting heavily, happy and excited from the hike. It was our first vacation after the dog attack, one year later.

We had discovered Crazy Woman Canyon through an encounter with a police officer. We had stopped at a truck stop near Gillette, Wyoming to take showers, and stock up on supplies. It was a bright afternoon illuminated by crystal clear Western sunlight. Anne was inside the truck stop taking her shower, and I was out in the parking lot arranging our stuff in the back of our van. Suddenly, I looked up and saw a police car slowly approaching me.

Wyoming is an extremely conservative state culturally and politically, as much of a red state as Texas. With my long hair and Anne's bright red hair and turquoise colored horn rimmed glasses, we were getting a lot of *"you're not from around here"* looks from the locals. When I saw the squad car approaching me I thought to myself, *"Oh shit, some Wyoming redneck cop is going to hassle me because I look like a hippie!"*

"You've been out in this parking lot a long time," the officer said as he got out of his car. "What are you doing here?"

"We're just tourists from Chicago," I explained to him. "My wife and I are camping nearby, and we're just cleaning up and buying supplies. My wife's in the truck stop taking a shower."

The officer seemed to be satisfied with my explanation, and once he decided I was not suspicious he turned out to be a nice guy. He pulled a large, detailed, topographical map of the region out of his glove compartment, spread it out on the hood of the cop car, and started telling me about the best places to hike and camp in the area.

As he was doing so, Anne came out of the truck stop having finished her shower. I saw her over the cop's shoulder across the parking lot, and the expression on her face was priceless. By that time, I knew that everything was fine with the officer, but Anne had no way of knowing that, and her face dropped when she saw me talking to him. I had to bite my cheeks to keep from laughing.

"You should camp in Crazy Woman Canyon, it is beautiful!" the officer told us when Anne came over.

"Oh, I'm there!" Anne said immediately raising her hand and we all laughed. The cop was right, Crazy Woman Canyon turned out to be stunningly beautiful, and we spent most of our vacation camping there.

There were two different legends about who Crazy Woman was, and nobody knew if either of them was true. One claimed that Crazy Woman was a white frontier woman who went mad when she saw her husband killed in front of her by Sioux and Cheyenne warriors. The other story was that she was a Native American woman who lived alone in the canyon. She shot the rapids of the river in her canoe on full moon nights and was said to have other mystical powers. Anne and I preferred the second version.

While the identity of Crazy Woman in Wyoming remained a historical mystery, there was no doubt about who Crazy Woman was in our lives. Lizzie was the most bat shit crazy woman we had ever met, and we had been through a war with her for the prior year. Anne and I found it a hilarious irony that our first vacation after the dog attack was spent in Crazy Woman Canyon after an encounter with a police officer.

"We can't even go on vacation without police presence!" we said to each other laughing. During the past year we had more contact with the police and the legal system than during the entire rest of our lives put together, and we had survived the war with Lizzie and Wade. After the year we had just lived through, there could have been no more appropriate vacation destination than Crazy Woman Canyon.

A poignant road trip moment came at Badlands National Park in South Dakota. We took a driving tour on a loop through the Badlands, which are arid, stark rock formations which look primeval. The rock formations were chalk white, almost the same color as Anne's scars. We stopped at a scenic overlook to take pictures, and there were a lot of other tourists doing the same. We were taking pictures of each other at the scenic overlook, and Anne was wearing a t-shirt which covered her shoulder scars.

"I want to take a sleeveless picture," Anne suddenly told me. She whipped off her t-shirt and was wearing a dark blue, sleeveless tank top underneath. She confidently leaned against the guard rail, and I took a picture of her, with a lot of other tourists nearby. She said later she caught some of the other tourists looking at her shoulder scars, but she did not care.

It is a beautiful picture of Anne. She smiles beautifully into the camera and the sunlight highlights her bright red hair, windblown from camping and hiking, which stands out in bold relief against the clear blue desert sky. In the background, the vast, primeval landscape of the Badlands recedes into the distance, and the brilliant, intense desert sunlight hits directly on the scars of Anne's right shoulder.

It strikes me as symbolically appropriate that this picture is taken in a place called the Badlands. Throughout the year after the dog attack we felt like we had been traveling through the Badlands, as though we were on a long, dark journey through a harsh, unforgiving wilderness. We had survived and emerged on the other side. This picture of Anne in the Badlands makes me feel as if we were finally emerging from the darkness and into the light.

MOVING ON

You Can Only Lose What You Cling To.
Buddha.

Over two years after the dog attack, I stumbled across some photographs of our old yard, which were beautiful photographs of the roses Anne had planted. We had taken numerous photographs, close up shots of our roses, silhouetted against dramatic cloud formations which glowed a pale yellow from the evening sun. They were taken shortly after a rain-storm and drops of water glistened on our rose petals. These photographs were time stamped on Sunday, four days before the dog attack.

Looking at these photographs two years later, I realized that this was the last evening we ever spent together in the back yard we loved so much. We usually only worked in our yard on weekends, because we were too busy during the work week, so Sunday June 16th would have been the last evening. The next weekend Anne was in the hospital. Two weekends later, the fight with Lizzie and Wade occurred, our relationship with them had turned ugly and we stopped going in our yard because of the threat from them.

A couple of the photographs we did not like, because they showed Lizzie and Wade's tall balcony in the background. Even when we were friendly with them, we considered this balcony an eyesore and it loomed ominously in the background of the photographs with stark ugliness. Soon afterward the balcony would become a dark stage for their threats and abuse.

We did not always take photographs in our yard, but we did so on that evening. Why did we pick that night to take photographs? Maybe it was just a coincidence, but I wondered if we had some subconscious premonition of what was going to happen, that our lives would soon be changed forever. Looking at these photographs, I had the same feeling as when I had re-read my email exchange with Jeanine about a lunch order written on the day of the attack. Like those emails, the photographs of the roses were an eerie and haunting snapshot of our lives as they existed shortly before the dog attack. Although we did not realize it at the time, when Anne and I took those photographs of our yard, we were saying goodbye.

"Look at the date these pictures are time stamped," I said to Anne, pointing at the stamp. "That's the last weekend in our yard before the attack."

Anne was downloading some of the photographs to make a calendar. She is not nearly as sensitive to dates and years as I am, and she had not noticed the date when the photographs were time stamped. When I pointed this out to her, she put both hands over her mouth, gasping in disbelief. Softly, under her breath, she said, "They took so much away from us."

Our tenants' lease was due for renewal in August, and I wanted to go inspect the old house and have our tenants sign the new lease. For obvious reasons, I did not like to go to the old house, but I wanted to see how our tenants were keeping the place, so I texted them and scheduled a visit at 8am on a weekday.

"You don't have to go over there. There's no specific reason. You can just email them the lease," Anne said to me. She worried that there might be an incident with Lizzie and Wade, because they did not see me every day any more and they would take advantage of their limited opportunity to attack me.

"I know," I replied. "But I haven't been over there in a year. I want to see how these guys are keeping the place up."

Prior to the visit, I stopped by a hardware store to pick up a fresh canister of pepper spray. The old canister was over three years old, and I was not sure if it would still work if I needed it. Ironically, I found it much more difficult to go to the old house when I only had to go occasionally, as opposed to during our move when I went there almost every day. During the move, I was constantly in a tense, hyper-vigilant, negative state of mind. It was difficult for Anne to live with, but necessary for my mental and emotional survival. Now that the move was over, I was much more relaxed, happy, and easy going. It was difficult, if not impossible, to turn on the old war mindset for just one morning to visit the old house, and I felt a lot of anxiety during the week prior to my visit.

Our tenants were young Latino brothers with long hair and beards who played in a band. When I inspected the house, I noticed a drum set in a corner of the basement which used to be my art studio.

"Is that where you guys do your band practice?" I asked our tenant, who replied yes.

"I did my artwork in that space for years," I told him. "I'm glad you guys are still using it as a creative space. That's nice, I like that!"

As much as possible, I tried to keep Anne out of the rental business and handle all the affairs myself. I met with our tenants to collect the rent and called repair and maintenance people as needed. The old house was next door to a crime scene for Anne, and I worried that dealing with its business would traumatize Anne and aggravate her PTSD. Sometimes it was unavoidable that she would have to get involved, but I did everything I could to protect her from the situation.

During the summer, Anne received a text message from Lizzie saying, "*Your tenants are becoming a problem! I'll be starting to call the cops on them And if they have a huge party on the 4th of July we'll be calling the police on you!*"

It had been almost two years with no incident with Lizzie and Wade, but suddenly they were back, rearing their ugly heads. We would be happy if they called the police on us as it would give us an opportunity to tell the police our background history and our concerns about security on the block. We figured the more police presence, the better. The Chicago Police Department could have set up a headquarters in the factory across the street and we would have been thrilled. Friends suggested that Anne have Lizzie's number blocked, but we chose not to because we wanted to receive any calls or text messages from her for legal reasons. If she texted Anne any specific threats we wanted to have a record of it so we would have evidence if we ever needed to take them to court again.

"Last week I got in a shouting match with that lady who lives next door!" our tenant told me when I met with him to collect rent, "I was just moving a bag of dirt out in the yard and she opened her window and started screaming derogatory shit at me! Then her husband came out half naked and I thought he was going to come over the fence after me!"

"I'm sorry that happened," I told him after he finished describing the incident. "If they do this again, just call the police on them, don't even hesitate. We've called 911 on them before!"

I also told him about the incident where Wade had yelled at the Ramirez grandparents about where they parked their car, who did not speak much English, and he laughed.

"It was so stupid," I told him. "They didn't even know what the fuck he was yelling at them!"

Our tenant remembered our warning, saying "You were right, those people are assholes!" He handed me his rent money and turned to go back into the bar and grill where he worked. As he was walking away I turned back toward him and said again, "Seriously, just call the police next time don't even think twice about it!"

"I will do that," he replied as he went inside.

On New Year's Eve we received another nasty message from Lizzie about our tenants, this time a voicemail. It was a noise complaint about a party our tenants had shortly after 12:30am.

"I can't take it anymore!" Lizzie screamed into Anne's voicemail. *"If*

you don't get rid of your tenants immediately I will call the city on every permit violation you have!" We called our tenants to ask if there had been an incident with their neighbors on New Year's Eve.

"We had friends over on New Year's Eve," our tenant explained to us. "The wife came out and started screaming at us that we were being too loud. Then the husband came out and physically threatened us and he brought out buckets of water and started throwing them over the fence at us and our friends!"

"Wow?! Really?! What the fuck is that?!" I replied, laughing long and loud. "That water bucket thing is a new one even by their standards!"

"Here's what gets me," I said. "Its 12:30am on New Year's fucking Eve in Humboldt Park, and they're making a noise complaint?! I know what Humboldt Park is like on New Year's Eve. It's LOUD! People are shooting their guns in the air and shit! It's a loud neighborhood on major holidays like New Years Eve, Puerto Rican Fest, and Fourth of July! If you can't handle noise you need to get your ass out of Humboldt Park!"

"This is so depressing!" Anne and I said to each other after the incident. "I can't believe we're still dealing with this shit over 3 ½ years after the dog attack!" Property values had improved in Humboldt Park, and we would make a modest profit if we sold our house. We called both Jen and our attorney who both recommended we put it on the market this year.

In July, we emailed our Humboldt Park tenants notifying them that we were putting the house on the market. One of them emailed me back saying that he wanted to make an offer.

"I'm pleased that you sent this email." I replied. *"I was thinking that next time I talk to you I was going to encourage you to make an offer."*

The next week I met the two brothers at the house to inspect it and have them sign the new lease.

"Are you still getting any bullshit from those assholes who live next door?" I asked them as I was inspecting the house.

"Nothing major lately," they replied. "Just some dirty looks."

"That's one reason I hope we're able to sell the place to you guys,"

I said to the two brothers. "You know all about these assholes and you don't seem to be phased by them. You guys seem to be able to handle them. That's better than selling it to some new unwitting buyer who might not be able to handle them."

"That's one reason I would like to buy the place, so I can be a thorn in their side," One of our tenants replied.

"Yeah, we know how to put them in their place," The other tenant chimed in. "Really we just laugh at them now."

"Yeah, Anne and I reached that point with them too where we just thought they were a joke," I said.

I emailed Jen to notify her of their offer and explained how I wanted to sell to them because they could handle the evil neighbors. Jen replied with the following advice which echoed advise Anne had given me.

"I totally understand you're a good person and you don't want to sell to an unwitting person…but as Anne said, this really should not be your concern. Your wellbeing is first and foremost. You need to get the best price/terms and just get out from under this property."

I replied, "Yes you and Anne are right that this needs to be the best business decision for us."

Monday was the three year anniversary of the dog attack. At work that day another teacher warned Anne that a group of 7th graders had been talking about how they were going to jump Anne after school. The next day Anne made arrangements for a friend to driver her to and from work, so her car would not be vulnerable to vandalism. Her friend and school security escorted her in and out of school.

"I knew something was going to happen today!" I told Anne when she gave me the news. "When I called you this morning and you didn't answer I had a feeling something would happen to you on the anniversary of the attack."

"You have to get out of this job, even if you have to take a pay cut!" I vehemently said to Anne the next morning as she was waiting for her friend to pick her up. "This is taking it to a new level the writing is on the wall!" I was angry at Anne for staying in a dangerous situation, and I am sure my tone of voice did not sound good when I said this.

"Stop putting so much pressure on me!" Anne snapped back. She grabbed her purse and computer bag and stormed out without saying goodbye, slamming the door as she left. Anne was also angry at herself for being in this situation, and her anger resulted in her lashing out at me.

"I'm sorry I was negative this morning," I told Anne later that evening after work. "But I am really upset that this new threat happened on the anniversary of the attack. If it had happened any other day I wouldn't have been happy about it, but it really threw me for a loop that it happened on this day!"

"I'll give you that one," Anne replied. "It threw me for a loop too!"

At my next therapy appointment, I devoted most of the session to discussing my struggles to support Anne. I was completely burned out on her job, and the endless stories of violent abusive children and irresponsible adults in the administration.

"She's gotta get the hell out of there!" my therapist said when I described the incident.

"I told her that," I replied. "She got mad at me for putting too much pressure on her."

"It sounds like she doesn't want to see it," my therapist replied. I explained to her that Anne did not used to have a fear of change prior to the dog attack. She had changed jobs several times during her teaching career and had gone back to school for several degrees and certifications. I was historically the person in the family who resisted change, and I had stayed at my old job way too long. But now Anne seemed to have a strange inertia and was unable and/or unwilling to help herself. She had sent out only a handful of resumes to find a new job. In the past she had completed demanding degree courses while working full time.

Anne signed up for a real estate course to try to get into a new line of work but she was unmotivated and missed several deadlines. Anne had a good opportunity because Jen told her she would help her get a foothold in the business, but she seemed stuck in emotional quicksand, unable to take the necessary steps to protect and help herself.

The following weekend, we went to a concert with Jen at Ravinia, a beautiful outdoor concert venue which was an icon of Chicagoland summers. Jen was just as adamant as I was that Anne quit her job.

At the intermission of the concert, Anne told Jen about the incident saying, "I don't want you to judge me, but something happened at work I have to tell you about."

"You, of all people, should know that life can turn on a dime!" Jen told her. "You cannot keep living like this!"

"It's like God reached down and slapped her in the face!" I said after Anne had finished describing the incident.

"Yes, the universe is definitely sending her a message!" Jen replied.

"I need you to be patient with me," Anne told me. She reminded me of a point that her therapist had made, which was that it was amazing that Anne was even functioning at all as a normal person given everything she had been through.

"I need you to trust me that I am taking steps forward." Anne said, and her therapist was right that it was amazing that she had not simply dissolved into a grease spot on the pavement.

I did try to be patient with Anne and a year later during the summer she began to take steps forward. She signed up for a different real estate class which was much more structured than the previous class, an intensive course of five all day Saturday classes, followed by two tests. We both realized that the first real estate course was too open ended for Anne. With open ended projects, she often struggled to find her concentration and focus, but she thrived if given a firm outside structure.

"We both should have thought of that from the beginning!" I said to Anne. "We both know you do your best work when you have a firm structure and a tight deadline!"

Sure enough, Anne did much better in the second more structured real estate class. She studied like a dynamo and passed the first test, and as of this writing is studying for the second test. It reminded me of the Anne I knew before the attack, who once passed an extremely demanding education certification course called National Boards, while at the same time working and teaching full time. It was heartwarming to see traces of the old Anne back in action.

During Anne's first Saturday class, I was out of town visiting friends, and I called her in the evening to find out how it went. She talked my ear off for the better part of an hour about the class.

"How did Anne's class go?" My friends asked me when I was off the phone.

"It went great!" I replied. "Anne was talking like a machine gun! She sounded both excited and nervous. I haven't heard her sound that way in a long, LONG time!"

"That's so good to hear!" my friends replied.

My therapist made a great point when I told her that Anne had completed the class.

"This is so positive!" She told me. "Even if nothing were to come of this whole real estate thing, this is still a very important step for Anne to take! It's her first step to move forward!"

Three years after the attack, Anne's scars had lightened considerably and were not as deep. She had also gained back some of the weight she had lost after the attack, and her thighs had regained some of their former smooth fullness. One day she sat on our couch looking at her leg scars.

"No one will remember!" Anne cried bitterly as she studied her scars. "Not…one…person…will…remember!"

"Of course, people will remember Sweetie," I replied, attempting to console her, lightly stroking her leg. "That's why I'm writing this goddamned book! I will make sure people remember, I promise!"

I tried to sound confident when I said this, but deep down I shared Anne's fear, and I worried that I had just made a promise I could not keep. As the physical scars gradually faded and time rolled inexorably forward, what would the attack mean? Someday, the attack would be ten, twenty, thirty years in the past and we would move on to other issues. While it was nice to see the scars fading, the deepest ones on her thighs would probably never completely fade, and there was also a sense of loss because the scars represented a physical testimony of everything she had survived.

Deep down, I shared Anne's fear that the story of the dog attack would ultimately be forgotten. Part of my fear was that our story had no larger context. Many people have terrible experiences which are individual stories set against the background of a larger event, such as a war, a disease epidemic, or a natural disaster. Our story had no such context, and this made us feel that it lived isolated in its own bubble.

The dog attack would have no war memorial, no aids quilt to commemorate it. Why would anyone have reason to care about a dark, strange, twisted tale that ultimately impacted only two people? Anne and I both feared that we would end up alone in our memory of what we had survived and overcome, that our story would be meaningful only to us.

I planned to make an effort to publish our novel, but I was not looking forward to the process. Years of experience had taught me how tough it was to break into the art world, and I fully expected that the world of writing publishing would be equally tough if not more so. I knew I would be extremely disappointed if I was unable to publish it.

At the same time, I knew that with the *Eulogy in Pictures* series about my parents and *The Scar Dance* novel about Anne, I had written tributes to the three people I loved the most in my life, and I had done so to the best of my ability. I could be at peace with that. I would throw our story out into the universe and after that it was out of my hands, and the four winds could take it where they may.

Anne took photographs of our new yard on a beautiful, clear, full moon night in May. We had just returned home from a great concert, which was a tribute to Bob Dylan's 75th birthday, featuring several talented local artists performing their interpretations of Dylan classics.

Anne is an excellent dancer with a great innate sense of rhythm, and she regularly draws attention to herself when she dances. She had taken over the dance floor at the last family wedding reception we attended, and she did the same at the Dylan concert. The final act was a great band called Zydeco Voodou. Their lead singer was a beautiful young woman, blonde wearing a bright blue sequined dress.

Before their last set, the singer approached Anne and asked, "Are you going to dance during our set? We need you up there dancing!"

"Hell yes!" Anne replied, only too happy to oblige, and she and Jen danced in front of the band during their final set. Zydeco Voudou performed a great up-tempo version of the Dylan song *"On a Night Like This,"* with Anne and Jen tearing it up right in front of the band, the same friend Anne had danced with during the scar dance. After the show, Anne and I sought out the singer to congratulate her on her great performance, and she gave Anne a big hug, having made an instant new friend. *"Throw a log upon the fire and listen to it hiss, and let it burn, burn, burn on a night like this!"*

When we got home from the concert, a brilliant full moon hung over our neighborhood in a crystal clear, cloudless sky. Anne took photographs of the moon in our new yard, showing the neighborhood rooftops, with the white moonlight glinting off the telephone wires.

The new yard was much smaller because we had a garage, which was a Godsend because the extra storage space had greatly reduced our persistent problem of clutter. But we missed the expansive space of our old yard, and the high wood stockade fence which made it an urban oasis within the tough Humboldt Park neighborhood. The new yard had another improved feature, which was a nice covered back porch. On stormy nights, Anne and I loved to sit out on the back porch with a glass of wine, watching the lightening flare and listening to the rumble of the thunder. While there were tradeoffs between the old and new places, overall the new place was an upgrade. Looking at the photographs of the full moon glowing in our new yard, Anne and I knew we had finally made it home.